REVENGE ARC

Cat Voleur

Copyright Cat Voleur, 2023
Published by Archive of the Odd
Cover design by Grim Poppy Design
Illustration by Bri Crozier

Warnings

Murder, torture, stalking, exploitation, referenced sexual assault

ISBN 979-8-9884827-0-3

Folder paper texturing by SojanJanso on Pixabay
https://pixabay.com/photos/seamless-tileable-texture-cardboard-1807376/

Archive of the Odd
archiveoftheodd.com
@archiveoftheodd

Dedication

For Riley.

I will be dead when you see this, if you ever do. How I long to show it to you. But I don't want to spoil our ending.

This collection is a labor of love. Love for you. Love for our work.

I hope that in time, you learn to see it as I do.

I hope you know how beautiful you will be when we are finished.

Oh, how you inspire me.

Part 1:
Gut Reaction

Where the work of Riley Langdon
blossoms into more than just words
and our ideas meld into one.

The following is the first post from the Gut Reactions Review Account on Twitter, posted in December of 2014, and has been taken in its entirety. Alt text is included.

Gut Reactions @RileysGutReactions · Dec, 2014
Gut Reaction: Choke on Dirt (1978)

For a movie that prides itself on being too much, I was underwhelmed by the gore. The story was both lacking and slow paced. I mean, come on. We're all just watching for the revenge arc anyway.

5/10

[Image Description: Movie poster depicting a woman's back. Her clothes are torn and she clutches a bloody knife.]

💬   ⟲ 1   ♡ 3   ⬆

The following has been copied from a Tumblr account known as Deckland's Dungeon.

Deckland's Dungeon

| About | Ask | Submit | Archive |

A Blog Update/Upcoming Feature

Hello all freaks and Dungeon geeks,

Emery here.

I know you have all been waiting patiently for the

third and final entry of my Lisey breakdown as well as a beta review of ByteMe. Don't worry, they're still coming.

For now though, I am sitting on something that is just too special to wait any longer.

As many of you know, I was on a special recon mission over the weekend to take a crack at playtesting a certain roguelike from The-Developer-That-Shall-Not-Be-Named. If you follow me on any of my other socials, then you're well aware they bailed right out of AkaCon, leaving me high and dry in the middle of buttfuck nowhere, AL. (Still bitter, in case you couldn't tell.)

I made the most out of the weekend all the same. I met a couple of cosplayers from some pretty obscure fandoms that agreed to come onto the podcast for some specialty deep dive episodes. I hung around Artist's Alley and placed some commissions for the new avi that should be pouring in over the next couple of weeks. I also did quite a bit of networking, so hopefully we have a few new accounts reading this.

These are all standard convention practices for a dedicated businessman such as myself. What isn't standard is the panel I found myself sitting in Sunday morning.

Those of you who have been to an anime or gaming convention before know that all the big shots have basically already left by that final day. AkaCon didn't have that many big headliners to begin with. I was totally prepared to spend the rest of my morning hitting up some random Q&A panels for whatever fandoms struck me as the least offensive.

So you can imagine my surprise when I saw a Q&A panel for what is perhaps the most offensive fandom of all time.

Have any of you ever heard of Red?

It has enough of a cult following that I may not be surprised if one or two of you out there are fans.

It's well past time I did a deep dive into that one, I think. Not only is it the most successful horror webcomic to be hosted independently by an American creator, but the controversial content keeps it ripe for drama. And believe me, there's drama.

Now, for those of you who are fans, don't get too excited. There's no deep dive episode coming just yet—I've got all those topics scripted up through August. For those of you who aren't fans, I'm sorry for the rabbit hole I'm about to introduce you to. Consider this your final warning and don't blame me when you're 200 pages into Red research tonight.

Now.

Recording was expressly prohibited during the panel, but you know I have my ways. The audio quality is too poor to upload directly, but I'll be taking the liberty of transcribing the juicier bits for you throughout the day.

Some of you may be wondering at this point, who the fuck cares about some fan panel for the obscure torture porn comic? But that's the thing, ladies and gents, it was not a fan panel.

Riley fucking Langdon was there.

I hope I don't have to tell you all that she's a big deal. Maybe not in our little corner of the nerdverse, but I imagine there are plenty of you who have heard of her that weren't even aware of Red. Gut Reactions, anyone? Her casual commentary on Twitter blows my little tabletop community out of the water, and I'd wager her actual website brings in about twice the revenue mine does. And any drama lovers in my readership are sure to remember the 'Death Do Us Part' controversy. Remember that movie that marketed itself as a romantic comedy, only to feature a twenty-minute massacre at the end?

"The real horror of life is that it can happen to anyone at any time."

Classic.

She may not be as well established in the gaming and comic communities, but she is still a bonafide internet celebrity.

That is why I am so surprised and thrilled to bring you these direct, black market transcripts of The Red Panel.

I have the bulk of them typed out for you and will be posting the edited excerpts throughout the day while I wait for my weekly videos to render.

So stay tuned, and stay freaky.

-E

The following has been copied from the Red fan server on Discord in the #lobby channel.

lobby

Ami Gara
You guys will not believe what just happened

Simp4Scarlet
Wat?

InnocentTech
What?

Ami Gara
I met Riley Langdon!

Simp4Scarlet
Shut up no u didn't

SunnyViolet
How? When?

 HHMarch
Are you being serious?

 Ami Gara
Okay, well I didn't really 'meet' her I guess, but I saw her speak at a panel yesterday at AkaCon

 HHMarch
She wasn't scheduled to appear at AkaCon

 Ami Gara
She wasn't an official guest or doing autographs or anything
I don't think she was vending, either, or I def would have heard about her sooner
But there was a Red Q&A panel and she was just there

 Simp4Scarlet
U sure it was her?

 Sweetz
No way

 HHMarch
She hasn't been to a convention in over a year. Plus AkaCon is really small, right? If she could go, she would have been credited as a special guest for sure

 PoptartMaster
We have been BEGGING for Gut Reactions to tour

 HHMarch
Also, she lives up in the northern US. AkaCon would be a long way to drive

 Simp4Scarlet
Don't believe it

 Sweetz
Probably just someone cosplaying as Riley

 ShellE
Who would cosplay as a real person?

 Sweetz
It DOES happen.
And we have very few cosplay options in this community

ShellE
You don't want to chain yourself up and walk around the con naked?

 InnocentTech
How come we're not all doing our Red cosplays on OnlyFans?

 Sweetz
LOL

 ShellE
Dangerously close to creating a real red room at that point

 InnocentTech
Just saying, there's a market for it

 ShellE
Sicko

The following has been taken from the horror review site Bloodforblood.com in December of 2019.

Interviews

After Death Does Part Us: An Interview With Riley Langdon

Published December 2019

By Morris Kingsley

Last Saturday I had the pleasure of sitting down with writer and director Riley Langdon. She has just worked with DarkerFlame studios to write and co-direct the controversial indie horror film, "Death Do Us Part' which is making waves in the community online.

MBK: How long have you been working in the creative field?

REL: I guess about six years? I sort of don't like being asked that question—no offense. It's just sort of hard to answer. A lot of the hardest part of working as a writer gets done well before you ever see any money for it, and we live in a country where that's the standard of doing something professionally. I actually lost money my first several years writing. The system sort of bites creatives in the ass.

Shit, sorry. Can I say "ass?" Can I say "shit?"

MBK: You're all good.

REL: Good. I'm not used to doing interviews, still. I'm more of a Reddit AMA gal.

MBK: It could always be edited down, if need be. But we're a pretty informal outlet.

REL: You're not going to edit it down to make me seem like a psycho or anything, are you?

MBK: Not unless you say anything psychotic.

REL: I will try to be on my best behavior, then.

MBK: So has the horror genre always called out to you?

REL: I wouldn't say that it calls out to me, exactly.

I like to think of it more in the way that the genre chose me, the same way that a lottery winner might be chosen, but sort of terrible. Tragedies just seem to happen randomly in the world with no rhyme or reason, but once you learn to see that it's everywhere all the time, it's hard to look at much of anything else.

I was cursed, or blessed, with the sort of cynicism that allows me to just see potential dangers in everything. Horror is the only outlet I have that lets me share those thoughts without going totally crazy.

MBK: So you started with horror?

REL: I got it into it pretty young. But, I actually started writing fantasy, if you can believe it. Not the dark stuff, either, but honest to God, young adult fantasy. With fairies and unicorns and everything.

I have a lot of respect for the fantasy genre because I do believe it's the purest form of escapism, which I know is what a lot of people use fiction for. When I was young I used to dream about having a little forest lodge that I could hide in all day and write up all these fantastical notions I was always dreaming up.

But you know what a forest lodge is? It's a cabin in the woods. Semantics matter.

I think once you pull the switch on seeing the world in a menacing way, it's impossible to go back.

MBK: Is that where a lot of your inspiration comes from?

REL: Yeah, I would say so. I have always had a very overactive imagination and when it takes me to dark places, sometimes I just need to bring others along for the ride.

MBK: Was there an inciting incident? That flipped that dark switch for you?

REL: I see a lot of speculation online about how that switch got flipped. I think, because I'm very angry and very outspoken, people like to write this tragic incident into my past that explains those traits.

But no, I wouldn't say there was a singular experience that jumpstarted my obsession with the macabre. I was never attacked or assaulted or anything like that. Which is sort of amazing. As sad as that is to say—but statistically speaking, being safe is not the default.

I've been hyperaware of that, I think because I grew up in a very vulnerable position. I never knew my dad, my mom was never around, and I basically raised myself past the age of eight or so. When I started to be exposed to violent media, and was putting together that it wasn't all fiction, I started to realize that my upbringing was seriously dangerous and I would have been susceptible to a lot of bad things if they'd come along. So, I'm aware that I was incredibly lucky.

Now, it's sort of evolved, if that makes sense? There's this notion I resent: that something terrible needs to happen to a woman before she can understand the dangers of the world, or care about them, or even speak about them.

That's actually the sort of story I would want to tell to a mainstream audience if I ever get another chance: my preemptive revenge story. Probably still a novel, since I don't think any movie studios are going to want to work with me after this.

MBK: Speaking of which, let's talk about your movie.

REL: Right! The thing I'm supposed to be promoting. Or defending.

MBK: People are calling it the most controversial horror movie of the decade. What are your thoughts on that?

REL: I don't think it's true, but I'm also not surprised that people are saying it.

In an era of political correctness and trigger warnings, movie-goers are just ill-equipped to handle films that are hard to categorize. I don't mean to vilify those things, exactly, because I believe they have a place in publishing. I just haven't seen much of a cinematic equivalent. There are ratings, obviously, but you see an R and you don't know if it's for blood or nudity or language or whatever else. Audiences went into this without the proper expectations, and I can see why that caused a problem.

MBK: Did you not expect that you were going to have those sorts of issues with the press?

REL: Expect implies that I thought about it, which I really didn't.

This was a new medium of storytelling for me to actually work in. I feel like this answer is going to show a lot of my naïveté, but I didn't think about how to promote this to the press a single time during production.

It was a small indie film and I had the freedom to basically tell the story I wanted to tell. That's a once in a lifetime opportunity, and I wasn't thinking very far past that. And even still, I don't have a lot of hand in how the film is promoted.

Understand, that's not me trying to throw anyone under the bus. I gave them a grenade and no instructions. For all the heat that the marketing people are getting right now, they're getting people talking about the movie, and out to the theaters to see it. You have to give them credit for that.

MBK: So the box office numbers are doing well?

REL: Let's put it this way, initially there were not going to be box office numbers. We had not scheduled a theatrical run.

MBK: None whatsoever?

REL: Nope. We were just going to do festival premieres and then send it straight to streaming. Which, when you think about it, would have made the controversial part a lot easier to warn people about. Netflix has warnings and tags and stuff, that little MA pop-up for television—I think something could have been done. But the critics threw fits about it when it premiered and now here we are.

MBK: So the studio must be thrilled that it's taking off? No such thing as bad publicity and all that?

REL: Yeah, they're generally pretty pleased, but they're about the only ones.

It's very surreal. There's a certain level of dissonance that comes from being praised by the studio and creative team and having everyone else try to cancel me.

MBK: And I do want to circle back around to this, because I have more questions about the movie. But this isn't your first experience with strong criticism online, is it?

REL: You've got me there.

There were actually rumors that the studio hired me in the hopes of causing a controversy to drive sales.

While that's not true—I don't think it's true—I was approached for the project because the director had read another story I'd written that has gotten me into some hot water in the past.

MBK: And what would that be?

REL: It was—is—a little webcomic called Red. It's a very gory, over-the-top, violent revenge story that had a lot of people clutching their pearls when they finally noticed it. It's in its final arc now and scheduled to conclude this coming year, I'm already prepared for the pitchforks.

MBK: You do seem to enjoy ruffling feathers, don't you?

REL: Not really "enjoy" it. It's anxiety-inducing. I think when people are mad at a public figure, even a very, very small public figure such as myself, they tend to forget that we're real people.

I have strangers sending me the most vulgar, vivid death threats on a near-daily basis, and it absolutely takes a toll. Liking extreme horror as a genre does not make me immune to fear or anxiety.

But at the same time, it does make me kind of proud of myself. I strongly believe that if you're pissing off the kind of people who will take time out of their day to make those sort of threats online, you're pissing off the right ones.

My favorite kind of art has also always been the kind to push boundaries, and make people upset. So, it is sort of validating to know that it's what I'm creating now myself.

MBK: I think it would be hard to deny that you've pushed a lot of boundaries with this one. Do you feel cheated at all that the controversy seems to be centered around the classification of the movie and not the content?

REL: Disappointed, maybe.

Obviously I wish the conversation would be centered around the actual problem of gun violence.

When the concept was initially brought to me there was discussion of having it take place on a campus, which I was strongly opposed to. I was afraid that with a younger cast, we would be accused of contributing to the problem, politicizing it, maybe even glorifying the violence. It's frustrating to be accused of all of that anyway, even though we took it in a different direction. The last thing that any of us wanted was to distract from the real world problem that was being portrayed, and when you get the marketing team in the crosshairs, it feels like we may have done that.

MBK: Out of all the non-school locations in the world, what made you choose a wedding as the backdrop for the story?

REL: This is maybe the part of the interview where I sound like a psycho. It's a little sick.

MBK: Well, now we need to know.

REL: It was actually sort of a joke.

The idea spawned from my dislike of romantic comedy as a genre. My roommate–former roommate–and I had this ongoing joke about wedding movies being more interesting if there were a serial killer involved.

It was sort of a fun premise to goof about, but it did end up setting the groundwork for something really dark in this project, because it made a wedding seem like the obvious backdrop during brainstorming.

MBK: I would not have guessed that you hated romantic comedies.

REL: Because I'm a woman?

MBK: Because the majority of the film, while not strictly a rom-com, is a very believable romance with strong levity.

REL: Romance with strong levity, I like that.

I actually also have a lot more respect for rom-com writers than I used to prior to writing this. Our whole movie hinged on the audience buying the characters and their chemistry with one another before you get blindsided by the third act. I thought it would be a lot easier to do than it was. I had to scrap a lot of drafts, and ended up watching a lot of my least favorite genre of movie, which felt very ironic at the time. The biggest challenge in the script was getting the characters and the audience to be so invested in this big, glorified party.

MBK: You are probably the first romance writer to ever describe a wedding as a "big, glorified party."

REL: It's a good thing I'll be sticking to horror, then.

MBK: It's certainly good for all of us over here at Bloodforblood. Are you working on anything else right now?

REL: Nothing new.

As I mentioned before, my comic is coming to its inevitable conclusion within the next few months.

There's also my website, Gut Reactions, which is going to continue. The site itself is doing moderate traffic, but the Twitter page for it has really picked up now that I am a contributing participant in the film industry. For better or worse.

It was an honor to sit down and talk to one of the hottest new horror writers on the scene. I'm sure you'll all want to keep an eye on her, which you can do through her author site RileyLangdon.com or her review site GutReactions.com.

The following is a post made to the Gut Reactions account on Twitter in November of 2018. Alt text is included.

Gut Reactions @RileysGutReactions · Nov, 2018

Gut Reaction: Chastain (1990)

Perfect when in the mood for a classic. More visceral than the book (though with fewer spiders). This one absolutely holds up and is more relevant by the year thanks to toxic fandom culture.

8/10

[Image Description: Movie poster depicting a scenic cottage view on a piece of paper emerging from a bloody typewriter.]

💬　　🔁 22　　♡ 78　　↑

The following has been copied from a Tumblr account known as Deckland's Dungeon.

The Red Panel Transcript pt 1

{The following is a Q&A transcript from AkaCon's Red Panel, 2022. For the sake of ease I have abbreviated the names as follows, interview style: RL (Riley Langdon), PH (Panel Host), and A# (Anonymous person asking questions #___). The panel has not been transcribed in its entirety, the boring questions and bits of lost audio have been cut.}

PH: Thank you for coming everyone! We have a special guest here, Ms. Riley Langdon.

[Nervous cheers, rustling, surprised gasps.]

Thank you for joining us today as well.

RL: Thank you for having me on such short notice.

PH: This Q&A panel just got a lot more official than

I had even planned.

RL: Oh, please don't say that. I'm not supposed to put anything official on the books without Mila's approval.

[Audience chuckles.]

PH: It's a shame we couldn't get both of you then. But since we weren't expecting either of you, this is a huge win. I had a little introduction in mind that I was going to read—

RL: Oh, please. By all means, go on as planned.

PH: Alright. Well. Red, as I'm sure all or most of you are aware is an indie webcomic. It started back in 2015 and wrapped up just a couple years ago with its fifth and final act concluding in May of 2020.

Despite stirring up a lot of negative press initially and being largely debated by critics, the comic still has a strong cult following and dedicated fanbase—even in the anime community. Ms. Langdon—

RL: Please, call me Riley.

PH: Riley, do you mind if I ask the first few questions on that note? Just to get the ball rolling?

RL: By all means.

PH: Were you at all surprised by how the anime fans embraced your work? It's got a very western art style.

RL: I was pleasantly surprised that the comic was embraced by anyone, to be honest.

[Laughter.]

RL: No, but seriously, I think it makes a lot of sense. We hosted the comic online ourselves because of the nature of the content. And with a few notable exceptions, there were not a lot of independently hosted webcomics that were making waves like that in America at the time. We hadn't discovered the Asian webtoon market, and short of Iri's work, we were the only thing really pushing the envelope in terms of *graphic* graphic novels.

Anime fans are not only accepting of the visual medium, but there's a good subsection that likes the more visceral work we were going for.

Plus there's a large crossover community worked in with our original target demographic, which was the creepypasta fandom.

PH: I'm glad you brought up creepypastas. Were you surprised that there weren't more creepypasta or even more horror fans active in the community?

RL: I was at first. But creepypastas evolved to be more of an audio medium, far more than anyone could have guessed at the time we started. I think it makes a lot of sense that when you're used to listening to narrations and podcasts and even having streams on in the back, a comic may not seem as accessible or convenient for multitasking.

PH: But even in the mainstream horror community, you have a following.

RL: I have a reputation. It's not always good.

PH: Are you suggesting Red has not been your only debated project?

RL: That's putting it lightly. I think Red really set the tone for my career.

PH: Speaking of… I have just one last question before we open up the floor to the audience.

RL: Shoot.

PH: There have been rumors…

RL: There are always rumors.

PH: Is it true that you're thinking about a sequel?

[The room goes audibly quiet.]

RL: There is no sequel in the works. Not now, not ever. Someone leaked to a podcast a few weeks ago that I was meeting up with Mila, you know, the artist behind the comic. I really love working with them, and we've been discussing future collaborations. Very vague, very innocent, and and definitely not a sequel.

PH: I'm sure that's disappointing to a lot of fans.

RL: I understand. Believe me, I understand better than anyone. Red is its own, dark, sinister little world that I loved getting lost in for a short time. But I told the story I wanted to tell there, and Mila has expressed they feel the same. To step back into that, we'd only be muddying the waters and creating something less genuine.

PH: Well, I think we all hope that at least you get to work on something else together soon. But for now, let's open this up to the floor.

The following has been copied from the Red fan server on Discord in the #fan-theories channel.

fan-theories

Olive4

I am a big fan of the color theory. Even Langdon has said that the title of the comic, and a lot of the imagery that we

see in the color schemes, was supposed to be taken as a reference to the source material: red rooms. But keep in mind that the protagonist is actually called by the name they give her on set. "Red."
I personally really like the theory that there are different colored set rooms in the establishment. It hinted repeatedly that there are more sets, and I think the color coding of them would make perfect sense—plus it has that visual appeal that Mila likes to bring to things.

Sweetz
Have you read Violet?

Olive4
I loved Violet!
So sad they stopped updating.
I was already on board with this theory, but I thought it was really clever how the author went about it, and chose a color that could also be a name. Much more subtle.

Sweetz
Right?
It helped pay homage to the theory, while also keeping the same casual tone regarding confirmation as the original. Though, that's from only a couple chapters, so I wouldn't be surprised if it ends up actually showing the other rooms in between.

Olive4
Right, I don't think it's a coincidence that she used the last color of the rainbow to balance out the first color.

CreativeNotCreator
I had heard that Violet was actually based off of those notes that were circulating, you know, for the sequel that got scrapped.

Olive4
People have been citing those notes for everything for years...

CreativeNotCreator
Doesn't mean that it's not true.

Olive4
True, I just don't know if I believe it.

SunnyViolet
Yeah, Riley has been pretty clear from the beginning that she's never had any intentions for a sequel, I think those notes might be a hoax.

CreativeNotCreator
Or she's been going on about no sequels because she's upset that her notes got leaked.

Sweetz
Well, until she changes her mind about it, I'm willing to eat up all the fan content people are willing to produce.

Olive4
Same.

The following is a post made to the Gut Reactions account on Twitter in February of 2015. Alt text is included.

Gut Reactions @RileysGutReactions · Feb, 2015

Gut Reaction: Anon (2008)

Finally caved and watched this one. Would not call it a horror movie. The cat died.

Also have to wonder as a non-tech person if it's technologically sound? This depiction of the 'darknet' seems dubious?

Still entertaining (as a thriller specifically).

5/10
[Image Description: Movie poster depicting a woman's face displayed on a computer screen, the cursor lingering over her eye ominously.]

💬   ♻ 6   ♡ 27   ⬆

The following has been copied from a Tumblr account known as Deckland's Dungeon.

The Red Panel Transcript pt 2

A1: Have you ever been on the deep web? Like, for real?

RL: The short answer? Yes.

[Laughter.]

A1: Can we hear the long answer? Is that okay to ask, if I ask a second question?

RL: The truth about the deep web is that it is utterly, painfully boring. It's a fun thing to read about, and write scary stories about, which I guess is why people do it. It sounds like this obscure, terrifying, underground place where anything could happen, and that's just a breeding ground for horror, isn't it? If you've only ever been on the surface web, all the urban legends sound like they could be true.

But they couldn't be, and deep down I think most of us already know that.

The long story is that I found a cheap laptop that I didn't mind getting all borked up. I went through all the security measures. I had a more technologically-inclined friend put in more security measures. I made sure I was safe. And I hopped onto Tor to take a look for myself.

And like I said, the truth is that it's just boring as hell. You get to the secret wiki and it's just a bunch of unorganized links. Most of them are dead. Most of them take several minutes to load before you find out that they're dead.

I don't doubt there's some really fucked up stuff on there somewhere. But for the average person looking to get scared, I would say that reading about the deep web is a lot scarier than actually being on it.

The following is a post made to the Gut Reactions account on Twitter in August of 2017. Alt text is included.

 Gut Reactions @RileysGutReactions · Aug, 2017

Gut Reaction: Reprisal (2017)

Loved this one.

Not super believable in any regard, but highly entertaining. Gritty. They REALLY went for it. Has the sort of final girl you want to see make a bloody mess.

Appreciate the hell out of that.

9/10

[Image Description: A movie poster depicting a blood and mud-covered woman in lingerie, standing in the desert with a gun pointed at the camera.]

  18   45

The following has been copied from a Reddit thread posted in the r/writeresearch subreddit in February of 2015.

  **r/Writeresearch** Posted by u/RELngdn · Feb 2015

Has anyone on here ever been on the deep web?

20

Here's the situation:

I am working on a script based around an internet urban legend. I already know that the legend itself is impossible (and have already seen it be thoroughly debunked). I have toyed with the idea of letting the story just take place on the surface web in order to make it more realistic, but I want to do the original legend justice.

In that lack of realism, I was hoping maybe I could find someone familiar enough with the deep web to help me navigate and add whatever plausibility there is to be had.

Since it's obviously fiction anyway, I don't mind bending the truth, but I would love to include just a bit of authenticity to appeal to the nerd in me. Can anyone help me out?

Thanks,
—R

💬 16 comments   ↗ Share   🔖 Save   👁 Hide   ⚑ Report

Sort By: Best ▾

Slimewafflesurprise
Isn't the deep web where you get all those viruses n shit? No thx
⬆ 2 ⬇ 💬 Reply   Share   Report   Save   Follow

Jackthekiller
My cousin's friend went on the deep web once to buy some weed. Got super into bitcoin and is now totally insufferable. Feel free to include this in your horror story.
⬆ 2 ⬇ 💬 Reply   Share   Report   Save   Follow

SunnySunnyViolet
This sounds like an awesome project! Is it a book?

As someone who spends a lot of time reading stuff online, I have always thought that someone should try and publish a book about internet legend culture.

Unfortunately, I don't know anything about the deep web, but I hope I get the chance to read your story when it's done.
⬆ 1 ⬇ 💬 Reply   Share   Report   Save   Follow

Slimewafflesurprise
There are actually a lot of creepypastas published already. I recommend Citrus Decay.
⬆ 1 ⬇ 💬 Reply   Share   Report   Save   Follow

Brenda_reads_latin

Can I ask what the urban legend is?

⬆ 1 ⬇ 💬 Reply Share Report Save Follow

> **RELngdon** OP
>
> It's about Red Rooms. Allegedly you can find them on websites that host snuff films, or get invited to them directly by the owner. But they're basically interactive torture chambers where people pay in bitcoin to specify how a victim on the other side of the livestream dies.
>
> ⬆ 1 ⬇ 💬 Reply Share Report Save Follow
>
> > **Slimewafflesurprise**
> >
> > Red rooms r totally real
> >
> > ⬆ Vote ⬇ 💬 Reply Share Report Save Follow
> >
> > > **RELngdon** OP
> > >
> > > yeah?
> > >
> > > ⬆ Vote ⬇ 💬 Reply Share Report Save Follow
>
> > **Ralphdicated**
> >
> > Not sure you should be writing about that stuff, except maybe on r/nosleep?
> >
> > ⬆ Vote ⬇ 💬 Reply Share Report Save Follow
> >
> > > **RELngdon** OP
> > >
> > > Why?
> > >
> > > ⬆ Vote ⬇ 💬 Reply Share Report Save Follow
> > >
> > > > **Ralphdicated**
> > > >
> > > > I don't think there's any harm in writing horror stories. But I know there are some people who take those kinds of stories really seriously. You don't want to rub anyone the wrong way right off the bat.
> > > >
> > > > ⬆ Vote ⬇ 💬 Reply Share Report Save Follow
> > > >
> > > > > **RELngdon** OP

Aren't there people who take all kinds of stories seriously?

⬆ Vote ⬇ 💬 Reply   Share   Report   Save   Follow

○ **Ralphdicated**

It's the internet, so yeah, I guess. I just know a lot of people who write/read about that deep web stuff are total freaks.

⬆ Vote ⬇ 💬 Reply   Share   Report   Save   Follow

● **RELngdon** OP

I'll keep it mind. Thanks.

⬆ Vote ⬇ 💬 Reply   Share   Report   Save

○ **phdinterribleness**

Hi there!
Even though this IS for writing research, I wanted to ask if you had checked out the r/deepweb? I don't know how much of what they post over there is real or fake, but there are probably a handful of people who could help you.

⬆ Vote ⬇ 💬 Reply   Share   Report   Save   Follow

● **RELngdon** OP

Thanks, I will try that next.

⬆ Vote ⬇ 💬 Reply   Share   Report   Save   Follow

The following has been copied from a Tumblr account known as Deckland's Dungeon.

The Red Panel Transcript pt 3

A2: I guess mine is also a two-part question, and also related to the dark web. If you've been on there and it's that boring, I have to ask how accurate Red is? My second question is if you were worried at all about making so much of it fiction?

RL: Red is not very technologically accurate at all, really. Ultimately I decided it was more important to keep the core legend alive than stress what is and is not possible with the limitations of the deep web.

But I'll be the first to admit that it worried me. Especially early on in the process. In the original idea we had wanted to go a more realistic route than the standard deep web fare. It wasn't until a little later in when that fell apart anyway that I felt comfortable taking more creative liberties. And at that point I decided I may as well lean into the pulp aspects of the piece to create the most compelling version of the story possible. I think that's what made the comic what it is.

The following is a post made to the Gut Reactions account on Twitter in May of 2015. Alt text is included.

Gut Reactions @RileysGutReactions · May, 2015

Gut Reaction: Mary Sue (2012)

Why is there not more body modding in horror movies?

Legit question.

Love the themes, performances, visuals, and extreme revenge. Not sure about the ending. Definitely could have pushed this idea further.

9/10

[Image Description: Movie poster depicting a woman in a black apron, arms crossed, a piercing gun in one hand and a bone saw in the other.]

💬   🔁 4   ♡ 16   ↥

The following has been copied from a Reddit thread posted in r/deepweb in March of 2015

⬆
48
⬇

 r/Deepweb   Posted by u/RELngdn • Mar 2015

Can anyone help me with some research?

Can anyone help me with some research?

I am writing a story based off of a deep web legend. I tried downloading Tor and doing some of the research myself, but unfortunately I have another person waiting on me and this method proved to be more time consuming than I had anticipated.

I could really use some help navigating the deep web or answering some of the specific questions I have.

The links I'm looking for:
- The original Lolitamaker site
- The Silk Road (or Silk Road 2, or whatever it's called now)
- Any sites with videos embedded
- Any site that takes bitcoin

The questions I have:
- Has anyone heard of the suicide game shows?
- Has anyone ever been invited (or know someone who has been invited) to take part in a red room?
- How many dead links did you have to click on before you found anything interesting?
- What's the worst thing that you've ever seen on the Deep Web?

Thanks!
—R

 36 comments   ↗ Share   ⊓ Save   ⊘ Hide   ⌓ Report

Sort By: Best ▾

TechAliv3

I think the Lolita site was taken down. You can still see the full image floating around the surface web though, if I'm thinking of the right thing.

⬆ 6 ⬇ 💬 Reply Share Report Save Follow

> **Lichotomy9**
>
> Yeah, a lot of the sites you mentioned were taken down. There are a lot of clones of Silk Road, but they're all pretty sketchy. (More so than the original, even.)
>
> ⬆ 2 ⬇ 💬 Reply Share Report Save Follow

Dead0a

Cheese pizza

⬆ 5 ⬇ 💬 Reply Share Report Save Follow

> **WinchesterActive**
>
> No way in hell you ever saw any cheese pizza
>
> ⬆ 4 ⬇ 💬 Reply Share Report Save Follow

> > **Dead0a**
> >
> > no way in hell you've ever spent any time on the deep web and NOT seen some cheese pizza
> >
> > ⬆ 6 ⬇ 💬 Reply Share Report Save Follow

> > > **RELngdon** OP
> > >
> > > Cheese pizza?
> > >
> > > ⬆ 2 ⬇ 💬 Reply Share Report Save Follow

> > > > **WinchesterActive**
> > > >
> > > > Don't listen to him, OP, it's disgusting.
> > > >
> > > > ⬆ 2 ⬇ 💬 Reply Share Report Save Follow

> > > > > **Dead0a**
> > > > >
> > > > > yeah, and the deep web is crawling with it
> > > > >
> > > > > ⬆ 3 ⬇ 💬 Reply Share Report Save Follow

> > > > > > **WinchesterActive**
> > > > > >
> > > > > > If I really thought you'd seen any, I'd report you.
> > > > > >
> > > > > > ⬆ 2 ⬇ 💬 Reply Share Report Save Follow

Dead0a

i didn't look it up or anything. But there's no way to know what you're clicking on. I said it was the worst thing I've ever seen on there.

⬆ 1 ⬇ 💬 Reply Share Report Save Follow

 **RELngdon** OP

Still not sure I know what this means?

⬆ 1 ⬇ 💬 Reply Share Report Save Follow

 **WinchesterActive**

Well, think of the worst thing you can with those initials.

⬆ 2 ⬇ 💬 Reply Share Report Save

⬤ **RELngdon** OP

Ah, got it.

⬆ 1 ⬇ 💬 Reply Share Report

⬤ **DreadPirateNothing**

Red rooms do not exist, OP.

⬆ 4 ⬇ 💬 Reply Share Report Save Follow

⬤ **House8blt**

Same with the suicide shows

⬆ 2 ⬇ 💬 Reply Share Report Save Follow

⬤ **RELngdon** OP

I heard people still get invited to them, though. Most likely scammed. Is this not true?

⬆ 2 ⬇ 💬 Reply Share Report Save Follow

⬤ **DreadPirateNothing**

Not that I have ever encountered.

⬆ 3 ⬇ 💬 Reply Share Report Save Follow

⬤ **House8blt**

This may have happened years ago, but people wisened up. Videos don't render fast enough for streaming to be a viable option. Once you'd been on the deep web long enough, you'd be able to spot a scam like that easy.

⬆ 2 ⬇ 💬 Reply Share Report Save Follow

> **TechAliv3**
> And bitcoin isn't what it used to be either.
>
> ⬆ 1 ⬇ 💬 Reply Share Report Save Follow
>
> > **number1birch**
> > crypto bros ruin everything
> >
> > ⬆ 6 ⬇ 💬 Reply Share Report Save Follow

Greenplatinum
I saw some dead bodies on the deep web once.

⬆ 3 ⬇ 💬 Reply Share Report Save Follow

> **RELngdon** OP
> Do you remember where?
>
> ⬆ 2 ⬇ 💬 Reply Share Report Save Follow
>
> > **Greenplatinum**
> > No, sorry. I was just clicking through some of the links when I found them. They looked sorta grainy, like the resolution was real bad. But I'm pretty sure they were legit.
> >
> > ⬆ 1 ⬇ 💬 Reply Share Report Save Follow
> >
> > > **RELngdon** OP
> > > Were they crime scene photos?
> > >
> > > ⬆ 1 ⬇ 💬 Reply Share Report Save Follow
> > >
> > > > **Greenplatinum**
> > > > War crime scene photos maybe? I remember one guy's face was real messed up, like it had been burned or something.
> > > >
> > > > ⬆ 1 ⬇ 💬 Reply Share Report Save Follow

> **WinchesterActive**
> Doubtful this was real.
>
> ⬆ 2 ⬇ 💬 Reply Share Report Save Follow

Lolorabbit89
The scariest thing I ever saw on the deep web was that Lolita site that you mentioned. Now I know it's just a hoax, but I didn't for a

long time. That shit gave me nightmares.

Even now I still have to wonder who would come up with that kind of a story.

I have a screen cap of the page if you want me to send it.

⬆ 2 ⬇ 💬 Reply Share Report Save Follow

> ● **RELngdon** OP
> That would be very helpful, thank you.
>
> ⬆ 1 ⬇ 💬 Reply Share Report Save Follow
>
> > ● **WinchesterActive**
> > It's probably just that same pic that you've seen floating around the surface web.
> >
> > ⬆ Vote ⬇ 💬 Reply Share Report Save Follow

● **Darkcranks**
Have you ever played The Game Starts Here?

⬆ 1 ⬇ 💬 Reply Share Report Save Follow

> ● **RELngdon** OP
> No, what is that?
>
> ⬆ 1 ⬇ 💬 Reply Share Report Save Follow
>
> > ● **Darkcranks**
> > $10 on Steam. Basically like a deep web sim
> >
> > ⬆ 1 ⬇ 💬 Reply Share Report Save Follow
> >
> > > ● **RELngdon** OP
> > > Not sure that it will help, but definitely worth checking out. Thanks.
> > >
> > > ⬆ 1 ⬇ 💬 Reply Share Report Save Follow
> > >
> > > > ● **Darkcranks**
> > > > Np
> > > >
> > > > ⬆ 1 ⬇ 💬 Reply Share Report Save Follow

● **Hookhandmassacre**
Once I was on the deep web and the creepy surgeon man asked me to give him a bitcoin. But when I did he FOUND MY HOUSE AND THEN I DIED.

Vote ⬇ 💬 Reply Share Report Save Follow

GemmaGames
Most of the sites that have videos are the ones you don't want to visit. Same with the ones that take bitcoin these days. Hope you're using a cheap computer.

Vote ⬇ 💬 Reply Share Report Save Follow

New Post: The_Creat0r

The worst thing I've ever seen on the deep web was a page for your comic, R, the criticism on it.

I didn't take too kindly to the way some people will discuss your great work.

The following has been copied from a Tumblr account known as Deckland's Dungeon.

The Red Panel Transcript pt 14

A13: You've said before on your blog that you did a lot of research before you started writing Red. Did you enjoy it?

RL: What a question.

I think to do any kind of research for a creative project, especially an unpaid creative project, it has to be something you're really passionate about.

But 'enjoy' is a weird word.

I think you might have to be sort of a sick person to really enjoy the sort of content I was consuming when I put the outline together.

The following is a post made to the Gut Reactions account on Twitter in April of 2016. Alt text is included.

 Gut Reactions @RileysGutReactions · April, 2016

Gut Reaction: Interview (1999)

On a hot streak with these foreign films.

Slow burn with a splattery finish. Adored the acting, the effects, and the constant hint of something darker happening just beneath the surface.

8/10

[Image Description: Movie poster depicting a woman looking back over her right shoulder at the camera, with a syringe in her left hand.]

⟳ 22   ♡ 78   ↑

The following has been copied from a Tumblr account known as Deckland's Dungeon.

The Red Panel Transcript pt 4

A3: Were you disappointed that Mila wouldn't draw all the stuff from the script?

[There is a long, uncomfortable pause.]

RL: Mila drew everything from the final version of my script.

A3: I heard there were deleted scenes.

[Another pause, audience murmuring.]

RL: The thing about comics is that they're a

collaboration between the writer and the artist. Mila never refused to draw anything, but I listened to them about what they thought would be most effective on the page.

It went both ways.

There were times I gave them feedback on designs for foreshadowing and narrative purposes. But there were also times they gave me feedback, visually speaking. I wouldn't say that they refused to draw stuff. It was our script. We worked on it together.

The following is a private email correspondence from December 2019 between Mila and Riley.

Subject: Revisions

From: Mila <MilaStudios@gmail.com>
To: Riley <RELangdon13@gmail.com>

Hey there,

So I had a couple questions/concerns about the upcoming pages that I wanted to address with you.

I know that when we started talking about this project together the idea was to push the limits of what had been done with this kind of story. Hold nothing back, show all the violence, etc.

I think we can still make good on that promise, while also reeling it back just a bit.

Attached are a couple notes I had regarding revisions for the next chapter that I think make the scene more palatable.

Sincerely,
Mila

Subject: Re: Revisions

From: Riley <RELangdon13@gmail.com>
To: Mila <MilaStudios@gmail.com>

Mila,

I looked over your notes and I have to say I'm surprised.

You know I'm always open to your criticism on the script, but as you said in your last email, our goal was to push the boundaries of what had been done with this kind of story. I'm sure I don't have to tell you this, but there is a lot that has been done with this exact kind of story—even in the years since we've started this. If we're not pushing hard, there's going to be nothing separating us from the others.

—R

Subject: Re: Revisions

From: Mila <MilaStudios@gmail.com>
To: Riley <RELangdon13@gmail.com>

Riley,

I don't think that's true.

Remember we looked over a lot of the inspiration material for this together back when we did character designs, and started storyboarding, and I think there's plenty of room to push boundaries without being quite as explicit.

One thing that separates us already is that we're releasing this as a visual format. With the exception of one or two lower-budget projects, no one has committed to showing what most people just tell.

The script you sent would be explicit, even if this were just another deep web creepypasta—and it's not. That's not what we're doing here. This would be leaps and bounds above what anyone else has shown in a comic of this nature.

—Mila

Subject: Re: Revisions

From: Riley <RELangdon13@gmail.com>
To: Mila <MilaStudios@gmail.com>

Don't you want to be leaps and bounds ahead of everyone else?

Subject: Re: Revisions

From: Mila <MilaStudios@gmail.com>
To: Riley <RELangdon13@gmail.com>

Riley,

I think this might be more than people are willing to read. To put it bluntly, there's content in here that I would be uncomfortable drawing.

Subject: Re: Revisions

From: Riley <RELangdon13@gmail.com>
To: Mila <MilaStudios@gmail.com>

It's not supposed to make you comfortable. I think if we're comfortable with everything we're doing we've lost sight of what we set out to do.

Subject: Re: Revisions

From: Mila <MilaStudios@gmail.com>
To: Riley <RELangdon13@gmail.com>

If I'm uncomfortable, how the hell do you think readers are going to feel when they log onto our site and see this in full color?

Subject: Re: Revisions

From: Riley <RELangdon13@gmail.com>
To: Mila <MilaStudios@gmail.com>

Scared.

I think their skin is going to crawl and I think that's exactly what we want it to do.

I want it to be uncomfortable, and I want it to stay that way. How many comics have been made on the cusp of trends, only to become memes just a few years later?

Ce trou a toujours été le mien!

People aren't going to be doing that shit with this. They aren't going to want to, because we're going to stick the landing.

I get what you're saying, Mila, I really do.

But THIS is the direction that media is headed in.

If we don't do this now, someone else is going to in another 5, 10, 15 years. We can either lay the groundwork for the extreme stuff, or we can be the enduring standard by which all this sort of content is eternally measured.

Would you rather create Camp Blood? Or the Deep South Slaughter?

Subject: Re: Revisions

From: Mila <MilaStudios@gmail.com>
To: Riley <RELangdon13@gmail.com>

Deep South Slaughter.

But you're steering away from that and into some Bolivian Footage territory.

If we push the readers so far into discomfort that it's all they remember, they're not going to care about everything we've been building to up until this point. The setting, the world building, the characters—none of it will matter. We're going to be a shock comic, graphic for the sake of being graphic, and no one is going to remember all the work we've put in. That you have put in.

Riley, I think this story is great. You're a fantastic writer and it's why I agreed to work with you in the first place. But there is such a thing as too much, and we are dangerously close to that line right now.

How much blood do you actually see in DSS? Hm?

Or did it work because a lot of the actual violence was left to the imagination of the audience?

Even if I wanted to draw these things, and you know I don't, there's nothing I can put in that's going to be scarier than what the audience can imagine.

I think you know that.

Subject: Re: Revisions

From: Mila <MilaStudios@gmail.com>
To: Riley <RELangdon13@gmail.com>

Is this about the incident at ComicVerse?

When I told you that I didn't need you to defend me, it wasn't a suggestion that we needed to push the audience even further. Only that I can hold my own.

I appreciated the intention, and I wasn't trying to push you away.

Subject: Re: Revisions

From: Mila <MilaStudios@gmail.com>
To: Riley <RELangdon13@gmail.com>

Riley?

Subject: Re: Revisions

From: Mila <MilaStudios@gmail.com>
To: Riley <RELangdon13@gmail.com>

Riley,

I need you to answer me. I need to get started on these pages, and I want to know that we're in agreement about what should be in them.

Subject: Re: Revisions

From: Riley <RELangdon13@gmail.com>
To: Mila <MilaStudios@gmail.com>

I'm sorry.

I'm not trying to ghost you, I'm just frustrated.

Do the pages however you see fit.

Subject: Re: Revisions

From: Mila <MilaStudios@gmail.com>
To: Riley <RELangdon13@gmail.com>

Your name is on this thing too. I want you to be happy with what we're doing. This is your story.

I'm not trying to change your vision.

I'm trying to help you.

Maybe, if you're really unhappy with my edits, we can meet somewhere in the middle?

Or if need be, maybe we can find someone to step in with the scenes I really don't think I can do.

Subject: Re: Revisions

From: Riley <RELangdon13@gmail.com>
To: Mila <MilaStudios@gmail.com>

I'm not frustrated at you, Mila.

I'm frustrated because you're right.

I don't want the entire project to be undermined because the end is shocking. I'm going through that right now with the movie, and it sort of sucks. I just get so sick and tired of being the moral compass for horror content because I'm a woman, you know? It seems like when I go as big as I want to go, I'm a devil-worshipping Satanist trying to corrupt all the youth. And when I compromise, I'm just not as edgy as my male peers.

I feel like a man wouldn't have to think twice about putting this sort of shit out. You're right, it's going to be better because we thought it through, but I resent that I have to. And that if we did it my way we'd be accused of doing it just for clout.

Actual, real, human women experience this sort of shit every day but I'm apparently taking things too far by writing it down?

I'm just so sick of the double standard. Doesn't it piss you the hell off?

You've got to have it even worse than me. I've seen the sort of scrutiny you get on your social media for your identity, the things people say to you— and it wasn't me that was getting harassed at that panel. Isn't it infuriating?

Don't you ever feel censored?

Subject: Re: Revisions

From: Mila <MilaStudios@gmail.com>
To: Riley <RELangdon13@gmail.com>

I'm sorry.

I know that you're going through a lot with your work, and I take it it's not all going well. You've been in the spotlight a lot lately, and I wasn't thinking about that. I was only looking at this from an artistic perspective.

I'm not trying to censor you.

Do you want to do the pages as written?

Subject: Re: Revisions

From: Riley <RELangdon13@gmail.com>
To: Mila <MilaStudios@gmail.com>

No, I don't.

You're right, and I think your edits are fine.

I'm sorry I was a bitch.

You're right. I know you're right. It's just hard to back down sometimes, and I've been in a bit of a mood lately.

Subject: Re: Revisions

From: Mila <MilaStudios@gmail.com>
To: Riley <RELangdon13@gmail.com>

It's okay.

You're my bitch.

Attached are the rough pages, I'm going to try and get them inked this weekend.

Subject: Re: Revisions

From: Riley <RELangdon13@gmail.com>
To: Mila <MilaStudios@gmail.com>

They look great, Mila.

Thank you.

Really.

Subject: Re: Revisions

From: Mila <MilaStudios@gmail.com>
To: Riley <RELangdon13@gmail.com>

For what it's worth, I think there's going to be a point in your career where you don't have to choose between making art and making a point.

It was hard for me too when my stuff first started gaining real traction, and I didn't have a studio advertising my most sensitive work to critics.
Eventually, you're going to learn how to brush off the negativity and ignore all the assholes. You'll have to.

I'm just trying to do right by this project.

We want to make something that will last.

The following is a post made to the Gut Reactions account on Twitter in December of 2018. Alt text is included.

Gut Reactions @RileysGutReactions · Dec, 2018

Gut Reaction: Last House Down the Lane (1972)

This was fascinating.

Loved the subversion of expectations. Different kind of revenge format, to be sure.

Very ballsy to let both women die. Was not expecting what I got.

7/10

[Image Description: Movie poster depicting the storm clouds in the shape of a skull forming above a black and white, ominous looking house.]

💬   ↻ 31   ♡ 87   ⬆

The following has been copied from a Tumblr account known as Deckland's Dungeon.

The Red Panel Transcript pt 8

A7: Was Red always going to be modeled after you?

RL: No.

[Pause.]

RL: She wasn't.

In the original design, Red was actually different. We wanted her to have red hair and green eyes—that was how I described her in the rough draft of Arc 1. The concept was to give her features unique enough that Topher would recognize her instantly when she shows up at his apartment, even though he only caught a glimpse of her on the stream.

After Mila came up with the color palettes we went back to the drawing board for her. With the red lighting that is so prominent throughout, we felt like she may stand out more with darker hair. There was a similar thought process with the eyes.

So she wasn't really styled after me at all. I did reference poses for Mila a couple times, but I think any woman of around average height could have done the same. After we made her a brunette and gave her brown eyes, our options were really opened up in terms of models. I just happened to fit the bill of being pale and having dark hair that was long enough.

The following is a post made to the Gut Reactions account on Twitter in December of 2018. Alt text is included.

Gut Reactions @RileysGutReactions · Jan, 2021

Gut Reaction: Completion (2018)

Can't react to this one without spoiling it.

Won't even give you a rating.

Some things you just have to see for yourself.

[Image Description: Movie poster depicting the strings and neck of a cello, all covered in blood.]

💬   🔁 65   ♡ 189   ↑

The following has been copied from a Tumblr account known as Deckland's Dungeon.

The Red Panel Transcript pt 15

A14: You said that the deep web was mostly very boring. Was there ever anything on there that did really disturb you?

RL: I'm sure there is plenty of truly disturbing stuff on the deep web. But I never found anything on there that got under my skin. I suppose I'm incredibly lucky in that way.

Now what we have been building to. The following excerpt has been taken from The Site and is of the utmost importance.

Hello, all.

Welcome.

Hopefully you are already well aware of why you're here, and of our purpose. No doubt there are some strays reading, those who clicked in expecting only another dead link, but that is to be expected.

I welcome you, too.

I apologize for the formatting. Building a site for the deep web is, to put it generously, not in my wheelhouse. I will be looking to take on a couple web designers for the project, if anyone is feeling up for the challenge.

If you feel like this could be you, please, do use the contact form below.

I will also be looking to hire a tech person for hardwiring my streaming set-up, a hacker to run security, and potentially, a blacksmith to have on staff.

Again, if your skill sets fall within one of these categories, I implore you to use the form.

For those of you who are still confused as to what we aim to accomplish, let me ask you a question.

Do you believe that the world is all that it could be?

What about the deep web?

With technology being what it is on the surface web, a curious mind has to wonder why the other 90% of content may not be accessed as quickly and easily for the in-crowd.

For many years now there have been stories of what the dark web might look like, might be capable of. Many are horrific. Depraved. Nihilistic, even. But one, and I think you all agree, is a necessary means to an end.

Some of you may look at Red and see nothing but a comic rife with inaccuracies. I look at it and see the shadow of something that is meant to be.

I see a savior waiting to be born.

Red, the character, could not ever have become what she was without all the horrors she endured. We are on a precipice of having what the human race needs to set us straight. But the evils of the world may not be cleansed without first pushing the martyr to greatness.

I can create her.

I do not mind stepping into the role of villain so that a true hero will walk among us. If I do this, as you know I mean to do, with the noblest of intentions, am I not also a martyr?

I have the facility ready to do what must be done. I have a volunteer of sorts, to help me test the equipment before the time comes. I have the courage to try, and the calling to know I am right in my mission. I will not even flinch from the prophesied punishment that Red herself shall come to deliver to me once I have made her whole.

All I need from you is help with the tech.

That, and your attention. It is audience participation that pushes her over the edge, after all. By watching, you are now helping me in my holy purpose.

Who amongst you are brave enough to continue watching?

There are great things yet to come.

—The Creator

The following has been copied from a Tumblr account known as Deckland's Dungeon.

The Red Transcript pt 21 (final)

A20: Do you feel bad?

RL: Bad about what?

A20: There are people getting off to this comic. You have to know that. People who are inspired by the depravity you wrote. Do you feel at all bad about that?

PH: You don't have to—

RL: I'll answer.

The answer is no.

I don't feel bad in the slightest.

Men write about this shit all the time. Men get filthy rich off their gory sexploitation films where there's thirty minutes of assault for a flimsy slasher story that keeps the poor victim half naked until the very end.

It's hardly art.

There's no point, no nuance, no themes. Half the time it's nothing but corn syrup and an actress they pressured into showing her tits for the entire run.

So if you're asking me if I, as a woman, feel bad for writing about the same graphic violence and the actual psychological ramifications of that, then your answer is no. Not one goddamned bit.

But if you're asking me if I will take responsibility for the fans?

I won't do that, either.

The site features a strict 18+ sign in. These are grown ass people reading my comic and they are responsible for their own damned actions.

If they want to touch themselves to the blood and guts and gore, and treat my art like it's nothing but a rape fantasy, that's their business. I'd honestly rather them be on this screen jacking off than having them look at any of the real shit. Because that's out there too, and it's not that hard to find. There may not be any red rooms, or livestreams, but there is stuff online way worse than this that people can access. My comic is not the worst of it.

Even if, worst case scenario, Red was directly responsible for an assault, that would be on the conscience of the person who did it. Not me. You lay that blame at someone else's fucking feet.

[Silence.]

PH: I think we'd better go ahead and wrap it up there. Thank you, everyone, for coming, and thank you Ms.—Riley, for dropping in. If there's anything else you'd like to promote or—

RL: No, I'm done. I'm fucking done.

*The following has been copied from the Red fan
server on Discord in the #lobby channel.*

lobby

Ami Gara
I'm being serious, guys
It wasn't a cosplayer, it was her
She answered a bunch of questions from the audience,
and then she went off on one guy who tried to blame her

Sweetz
Blame her for what?

HHMarch
You haven't heard?

Part 2: Hiatus

Where the internet waits with bated breath to see what will happen next to our dear protagonist.

The world must go on in her absence.

The following text has been copied from a Yahoo! News Article.

Chained Body Washes Ashore in Elowen, OH

The corpse of a woman appalled and disturbed locals after being found Saturday night at about 9:00pm. Police have been reluctant to share details, but unsettled residents have been reaching out to express their horror and frustration.

Jeanette Irving, who discovered the body, was happy to comment. "It was like something out of a horror movie," she said, lighting up another cigarette. "Not just because she was dead, but because you know the poor thing had been murdered."

When pressed for explanation, Irving continued.

"She was all chained up. She had this heavy metal around her wrists and her arms were all red. Mostly she was bloated, and moldering already, but right around her wrists was all dark, like she's been burned up."

Irving clarified that she got 'as close to the body as anyone would' half believing it to be a Halloween decoration.

"It's a real shame that you don't know. People getting more and more sick with the stuff they display. But when you got close, you could tell for sure. Decorations don't smell like that."

Police have said that the investigation has taken top priority due to the violent nature of the crime in what is generally considered to be a safe area.

The following has been copied from Riley's Patreon page, a patrons-only tier post.

Going on Hiatus

Hey guys,

So.

This one is going to be sort of messy, and I apologize for that in advance. I didn't sleep much and I'm not really feeling myself, but I also need to write up a shorter version of this for my author site, and post something to socials. God forbid I ever take a break without alerting the world first.

Anyway, I won't have a lot of time to edit, I just want to make sure that I get you the information before I go, and that's more important to me than this last post being super polished.

The title pretty much gets the gist of it—I'm going to be going on hiatus. I don't have a set date when I'll be coming back. I'll be taking at least a week, maybe longer.

First and foremost, I want to reassure all of you about your status as my Patrons. I know there's a higher level of obligation from me wherever money is involved, and you may remember that's one of the reasons I dragged my feet about starting this page in the first place. That's not an excuse though, I'm still going to do my best to take care of it. I've taken the liberty of switching payments from 'monthly' to 'per-creation' until such time I am back to resume my regular perk schedule.

This, like my hiatus, is temporary.

When I come back, I will switch it right back to the monthly payments, but I wouldn't feel right accepting money while I'm not hosting the watch parties or uploading essays and perks and all the other things that you're paying me for.

I'll be leaving the various virtual tip jars open—mostly because I don't want to go through the hassle of deactivating and reactivating them—but I doubt I'll be checking them much. I just want to clarify I'm not asking for help by leaving them open. The community has already been really generous to me and one of my biggest anxieties is not being able to thank everyone properly in the way that you all deserve. That goes double for when I'm away.

Speaking of that.

I'm sure that by now most of you have heard about the case in Elowen. If you haven't yet, you will soon enough.

There are going to be a lot of rumors online and in the community about me and my work, and I imagine they're not going to get better in my absence. I don't know how comfortable I am talking about all these things, if I'm being honest, and this is in no small part why I feel like I have to unplug for a little while.

Still, it's hard to stay entirely silent on this.

You who follow me know that I'm not one to play it safe when I feel strongly about something, or when I think something terrible is going on in the world. I'm not really able to hold my tongue ever, and I guess this is no exception.

Whoever killed that woman in Ohio is a fucking monster. I do not now, nor will I ever condone violence. Not against women, or any human, or animals or anything. Just, no. Never.

Sometimes when writers write about things that get under people's skin, it is equated to actual, real-world violence. I have been saying for a long time that I believe this is wrong and that this attitude generally is not okay. Artists need to be allowed to depict the worst of the world. It's a form of catharsis. It's a form of grieving. When we start policing art or criminalizing creators, we take the focus away from actually fixing the real issues.

I have been very vocal, as recent as this last weekend, about creators not being responsible for their art once it goes out into the world, or for their fans.

I'm not suggesting or confirming that a fan of mine did this.

But it is difficult not to draw comparisons between the details of this case as they come out, and a certain comic that I wrote.

Logically, I still know that even if the comic inspired this, I do not bear the blame. I've always said it now, and if that belief is going to be tested, I am going to hold strong. My heart is a different matter though.

Despite what many people believe of me, I am not a person without empathy. My heart mourns anyone lost to violence, and I am struggling a lot with the idea that my words could have in any way inspired such poor treatment in her final hours.

It is a struggle that I mean to have alone, but I just want to clear the air before I leave.

I am stepping away for my own sanity during this time.

I don't have anyone advising me to do this. There are no lawyers involved, I am not involved in any official capacity, there's no team to pull my strings. I am a big girl and can make decisions for myself, I just want to stop those rumors before they have a chance to get going.

I believe, and I believe this strongly, that the internet is drawing lines between my work and reality where there are none. But since those lines pass straight through me, I just don't want a front row seat when it all goes to hell.

I need to take a little bit of time away. I need to get my head on straight.

Thank you for riding this out with me, those of you who will, and as always when there is an interruption, know that I appreciate your patience.

—R

The following is my first, and hopefully, last formal apology. It has been taken from The Site, and I found it fitting to include in this little side project, as I am now part of the narrative.

Hello,

I am sure by this point you have all read about the failure with my little experiment.

It is shameful, yes, but I believe that the correct thing to do is own up to it.

Though the first girl was willing enough in spirit, the human body is weaker than even I realized.

I want to clarify, I do not blame Riley for this.

Many times she has spoken about the difficulties that she experienced with her own creation; which things could be real and which things could be compromised. I think she found the perfect balance, but I know she did not get it on the first try.

Neither am I perfect.

With so few people stepping forward the operation here is smaller than I would hope. I am still bound by the same technological limitations that so constrained my muse—and obviously it would have been ideal to wait for a consultant with the metal.

I am learning that just because something was done in the comic, does not mean it is practical for our little homage.

Try not to think of it as cutting corners.

Think of it as uncovering the core of the story.

Does it matter how Red's chains were sealed? Or does it matter only that she cannot remove them?

It is the storyteller's prerogative to embellish such as they need to draw in an audience for the desired effect. Meanwhile it is The Creator's utmost obligation to overcome such pesky obstacles in the journey.

Still.

My greatest mistake was not the death of the girl, which was inevitable in either case. She was never special enough to be my Red, and did not understand how her compliance in the matter completely obliterated the point of turning her in the first place. In her version we would have been little more than play acting, because it is the transformation that will make the candidate special.

Had I been able to get the cameras running in time, I think you all would have rather liked how it went down with her, even. Yes, I think she would have liked to have the audience, and I think you would have liked to see just how much pain can be caused by something as simple as a festering wound.

The mistake was in the discovery of the body.

It has put things into motion that now, cannot be stopped. The only thing is to move forward and do the best that I can on a faster timeline. The final abduction will go smoother.

And this next one will be closer to the real thing, I think you all agree.

- The Creator

The following has been copied from the Red fan server on Discord in the #fan-theories channel.

fan-theories

HHMarch
My favorite theory is that The Creator was the one who requested Red

Olive4
It's an interesting one, for sure.
Can I ask if it makes sense?
Serious questions, but don't we see the message coming in on his computer when it comes in for the highest bid?

HHMarch
He could have sent it to himself

Olive4
Would he need to do that?

HHMarch
I'm not sure that he would NEED to, but I think it's plausible that he would
If the hints about the size of the operation are valid, there would be other people potentially seeing those messages, and he'd want her to look like any of the other girls to the staff. Keep her a secret

Olive4
That does make sense.

HHMarch
What I like best about it is that it low-key explains Red's special treatment.
Like, I know she has to make it a long time because she's the main character and there was more story Riley wanted to tell about her.
But in the world that's established, it definitely feels like she lasted way longer than any of the others and I don't think that's just random.

CreativeNotCreator
That's true. Even at the beginning of Arc 2 Red is surprised that she's lasted so long. Doesn't she say something like it's not uncommon for girls to die within the first month of being chained?

HHMarch
Yes!!! That's one of the first hints that we ever get in the comic for this theory. With the time skips in the flashbacks it's impossible to know for sure, but it's speculated that she lives in the facility for more than a year

Sweetz
A year seems plausible to me.
We see a lot of content during her imprisonment sections, and I'm sure that we don't see every minute of her time there. Plus with the healing of scars and wounds, there would have to be decent time skips between even the sections that we DO see.

HHMarch
The scars! Right
That's another thing I think lends itself really well to the theory
She honestly isn't terribly scarred

She has scars, but they're not bad. And a lot of people thought when the project started that it was just a stylistic choice, but there are other women that we see who have made it awhile, none as long as Red, who are more disfigured.

Mila is so consistent about that sort of thing, that I don't think it can be random

The idea that Red is having fewer disfiguring sessions and maybe even getting treatment between livestreams for her more serious injuries definitely implies (to me) that she's getting special treatment all the way around.

 CreativeNotCreator

But why do you think?

Is it hinted at anywhere?

Because to me, when I read his monologues, I always read a lot of derision in them. Like, he definitely thinks he's better than the men submitting requests.

 Sweetz

Would you be surprised that he was a hypocrite on top of everything else?

 CreativeNotCreator

Not exactly.

But I would be surprised if he was that obvious of a hypocrite, you know?

He has a reason for everything, I'm sure he'd have a reason why it was different for him to request her, even if it was a flimsy reason just for him—just so he could think he was the exception to his own rule.

Maybe he really believes she deserves it?

Or maybe he knows that if he can keep one around for a while he can cut back on the actual capturing process, which is the riskiest part for him?

I just don't like the idea he spares her because of something like a crush, when he thinks so little of patrons who choose women that way. I think he would need an excuse.

 ShellE

I actually did read a version where he didn't request her initially, but assumed control of her once he saw her pain tolerance.

The idea was that he had always dreamed of finding the

perfect victim, and he thought it was her.
I think this was almost confirmed in the end, even.
We know he has one secret he never got to tell her, and he's
mentioned more than once how impressed he was with her
"capacity for suffering."

HHMarch
I think that could also make a lot of sense. But it also just
feels like Riley would want to tie the beginning arc to the
end a little more concretely. That seems like it would be a lot
easier if the message we saw for her request had always
been from him because it would tie Arc 1 into that opening
for Arc 5

PoptartMaster
Would she be the one to tie it all together though? Really?
No shade but did you see her movie?

ShellE
LOL

HHMarch
That's sort of my point though? Riley as a creator seems to
take a concept and really run with it, regardless of what it is.
Red was something with a lot of clues and tie-ins and
foreshadowing. And even when you look at the coloring and
framing of the first panels in comparison to the last panels,
it's a very cyclical story
The movie was like, the exact opposite of that

PoptartMaster
No kidding there
But I see your point

CreativeNotCreator
I do like that The Creator request theory has so many
connecting rabbit holes to go down, like in regards to his
motives. Since it was left so open to interpretation, it's a
good kicking off point for other theories.

Sweetz
You're right about that

Olive4
I actually think the color theory and The Creator request
theory could tie directly into one another.

HHMarch
Yeah?

Olive4
Oh, definitely.
A lot of people think that if the sets are different colors, then the best way to rank them would be a ROYGBIV situation, which would make Red the top rank.

HHMarch
Ohhh
So you think instead of randomly getting assigned to one of the sets, he immediately gives her top rank from the beginning because he has chosen her?

Olive4
Exactly.
He even gives her the name of the set, which could be like, a ranking within a ranking, if that makes sense.
She's the Red of the Red Room.

CreativeNotCreator
There are also really elaborate variations (of the color theory specifically) that the colors determine what sort of torture was going to be happening on what set.

Olive4
Really?

ShellE
That has to be debunked already, right? Because wasn't that other girl—the super thin one in Arc 2, with the short black hair—wasn't she also intentionally killed on set?

CreativeNotCreator
I don't think it would be determined by lethality, right? Like, a lot of people obviously die on the red set, intentionally and otherwise. But that doesn't mean there aren't other kinds of torture which might or might not prove fatal depending on how far they go.

ShellE
True. But there would have to be some WILD stuff going on in the other rooms based off how much we see happening in this one
Assault

Audience Participation
Death
Bodymodding
Bugs
Torture

SunnyViolet
It doesn't really leave much for the other 6 rooms, does it?

Olive4
There could be something to support it though
Like, the lighting in the comic DOES change pretty
frequently. Red always seems to be a color for revenge in
the main timeline and torture in the flashbacks
What if the other colors also have meaning?
When she goes back to take on Rudy, remember how pale
the lighting was? There were all those blue frames right up
until the end
And when she found Madame it was red and purple

Sweetz
Plus all the green when she goes after Vic

Olive4
Yes!!!
They could all be some sort of callback to the sets

CreativeNotCreator
That would be some crazy storytelling if that was all planned
out somewhere between Mila and Langdon for a theory they
won't even confirm.

Olive4
It would not be the craziest background Easter egg that the
two of them collaborated on from day one

PoptartMaster
You're right about that

Olive4
I don't know if it's true, but it's a fun one to think about

CreativeNotCreator
I wonder if anyone has ever made a chart out of all the
colors in the deaths, and what type of revenge it
corresponds to.

ShellE
On it, lol

The following text has been copied from an RP account on Tumblr known as RedRedRed.

~~ Disclaimer OOC ~~
This is an RP account, not intended to be taken seriously. NSFW. 18+ ONLY
HUGE TW: bodymod, horror, sa, nc, gore, death, violence, abuse.
I do not own the IP but you can find the original comic here || LINK
Special thanks to MMMaru for the theme and custom color options uwu || LINK
~~
NOTE:
Obviously I'm super upset about Riley's hiatus. The RP will continue as planned, though. Now more than ever I think we could all use a little distraction to take our minds off everything that is happening.

The following has been copied from the Red fan server on Discord in the #lobby channel.

lobby

 SunnyViolet
So Riley's gone, huh?

 PoptartMaster
She'll be coming back

 InnocentTech
Yeah, but when?

 PoptartMaster
She'll be coming back.

 Ami Gara
The fact that she didn't set a date has me a little worried.

 SunnyViolet
She does have that deal with DarkerFlame to come back for, right?

 PoptartMaster
A lot of their writers are total hermits though

 ShelIE
It would be wild if the whole hiatus, and maybe even the thing with the body, were just stunts by the press to build suspense for the top-secret project she's been working on

 Olive4
Red the movie?

 PoptartMaster
This would be the wildest movie promo I have ever seen

 Ami Gara
Wilder than Kingdom of Blood dropping that huge-ass skull in the mountains for hikers to find?

 PoptartMaster
Not a movie
Plus they had all that blood money

 SunnyViolet
I would kill to see Red the movie.

ShellE
Literally?

SunnyViolet
Of course not literally, you freak.

PoptartMaster
I don't think they'd be the studio to pick up Red, though.
Seems more like a Z6 flick to me

ShellE
I'd watch either way

SunnyViolet
But seriously, do you guys think she's okay?

Sweetz
It's Riley. I'm sure she's fine

The following was posted to The Site within about an hour of me reading the previous discussion logged.

Hello all,

This is not my traditional post here, so I hope that you will bear with me.

But we need to talk about something important.

I believe there is a line to be drawn somewhere that separates fan content from greatness, almost to an extension of the original.

There have been books, movies, many different creations where the community has been a part of what has lead the original project to greatness.

Red was great on its own, of course.

Perhaps I might indulge, however, that my own extension of it was always to be from the beginning. That extension, mind you, is moving along well on its new timeline—better than could be expected, even, though it is not what I wanted to discuss today. Updates to follow soon, once I get a little further on my side project.

No, what I came here to ask was if there is also a point, on the other side of the spectrum, where fan content becomes disgraceful. Can something ever tarnish the name of something so pure? I don't think so, but it does sometimes seem as though there are people trying to drag down something beautiful, simply because they can never grasp it.

It is not, perhaps, for me to make these judgements.

Some people may even think of my own work as distasteful—I know Riley herself has had to put up such an illusion.

I think it should be up to the creator of a work to decide what is and is not an acceptable offering of one's talents in honor of the original piece.

But with Riley being offline... unable to make such a call...

One has to wonder who will step in to protect her words in her absence.

—The Creator

The following RP text has been taken from a roleplay account on Tumblr known as RedRedRed.

Red Red Red

About ∨

 blog-redredred

Red wakes up.

This time she isn't chained to the table when she comes to, but her manacles are attached to the wall.

She's scared, really scared, and she thinks that this time it's going to be for real. This is going to be the time that she's killed for the viewers. Something feels different as she looks over, expecting to see The Creator. Her eyes widen in shock when she sees the newcomer.

[OOC: go ahead, enter when you're ready.]

OC_Kurai

Kurai looks the woman over.

He is tall and lean with a surprising amount of strength in his wiry muscles; strength he hopes he doesn't have to use.
"I can save her," he thinks to himself.

But as he steps closer he cannot help but notice how beautiful she is.

[OOC: thanks! Never done one of these before]

blog-redredred

"Hello?" She tries to call out to this man, only to realize she is still gagged. Before she can struggle for her voice, she sees the stranger step into the light, standing before her in all his glory.

He does not look as menacing as the other men that have approached her.

She cannot think that he means to kill her...

But how can she be sure?

OC_Kurai

He knows the cameras are on him, and does not want to draw any extra attention to whoever or whatever is watching them. He does his best to look confident as he slides an arm around the naked woman. With his other hand he explores the metal that binds her to get a better feel for what he's dealing with.

blog-redredred

The familiarity of the gesture makes her try to pull away, but with the wall only inches behind her there is simply nowhere

She tugs uselessly at the chains binding her wrists above her head, and the ones at her ankles that keep her legs held open.

The chains are set into the wall, connected by padlocks to the permanent metal that encircles her limbs.

 OC_Kurai

"Don't be afraid," he whispers, so low that the camera can't pick him up.

"I want to help you."

He does want to help her, but he realizes to his dismay that he also just wants her.

He has never seen anyone so beautiful.

 blog-redredred

She cannot figure out his game.

Is this a new part of the show? If so, it is crueler than any of the measly tricks they had tried to play on her thus far. Still, with all she has experienced before, it is easier for her to believe that than the alternative, that he truly does mean to save her.

But perhaps...

Could it really be that she will have help when she goes on her mission of revenge?

The following has been taken from Archive of Our Own.

Violet

BloodyPurpleProse

Chapter 1

Violet knew that she was lucky in more regards than one.

Not only had she been given a very special place relative to the other girls, but it did not escape her that she had probably evaded a much worse life back at home, as well.

She'd been sixteen when they'd set out on the years long journey of fake agencies and border smuggling that had eventually landed her into the building she now reluctantly thought of as home. Already when they left she had been a shadow of herself. The little tricks that kept her from her mother's judgement and her stepfather's prying eyes were also likely the things that had allowed her to work her way to the position she now had.

She knew when to speak quickly, and how to obey. More importantly, she knew how to move silently and discreetly through the darkness, keeping her head down and not letting any unwanted attention land on her.

It had not been a perfect system.

In fact, she still bore a large scar that reminded her of just how tenuous her safety had been—and perhaps still was. It ran from her left shoulder, diagonally across her chest, where it curled around the base of her right breast. It had the faded, washed-out red of a wine stain, and was not so hideous to behold as when she had first been cut open.

Receiving it had been her own fault.

The first two shows—"streams," as they called them—had not been bad for her at all. They had all been presented as a group, all of them shackled and shivering, worried about what would happen. But both of those first two times, only one had been chosen, and she had been spared. All the bad things that had happened had only been to her mind, not to her body.

After all the things she had seen at home—war, poverty, violence—she had slept easily even with this new layer of fear added to the mix. She did not even struggle with the sniffles and sobs of the other captives that surrounded her.

Mostly they were other women, like her. There were a couple men among them, but they looked weak, malnourished. Violet imagined that the people who had taken them had looked only for those they considered easy targets. That was one thing they all had in common, none of had offered much of a fight. She imagined they, like her, had all seen their fair share of suffering, and that it made them similarly disinclined to seek out more pain.

Perhaps that was the hidden prerequisite for being there.

Of course, it was also possible that she was projecting her own history into the eyes of these strangers who spoke a different tongue than her, and whose stories she would never fully know. Regardless, she could see the shared fear in their eyes, and the curiosity about what the first strike would feel like when it finally came for them.

It came for them all in the third stream. That much was inevitable. Her mistake had come when they were permitted to choose their own instruments of torture.

There could have been worse choices, that was certain. A few had died that very night, and she assumed that any serious disfigurements might have disqualified her from the life she now led in the cage.

Her scar might easily have done the same, if people did not seem to agree that she wore it quite well.

She had not known then half so much as she had learned since. She did not understand which instruments of torture did which things to the human body. She had looked across the canes and paddles and curious metal devices, and her eyes had fallen onto the rack of whips. She'd heard some horror stories about whips, and the idea of choosing such a thing to be used on her had been terrifying. But it seemed better to go with the evil she knew than one she did not. She knew a lashing was not likely to kill her, and that was more than she could say about the other, unidentifiable items in the room.

So she had chosen one. The wrong one.

What she had not known then was that the thinner the whip, the deeper it would cut. The fewer the strands, the more exacting the slice.

It had only taken one lash from the bullwhip to bring her, bleeding, to her knees.

Violet would never make that same mistake again.

Notes:

Thanks everyone so much for reading!

I got into the comic super late, but was there to see the end and have been wanting to do something in the world since it wrapped up. Looking forward to posting more :)

The following has been copied from the Red fan server on Discord on the #fan-theories channel.

fan-theories

Capacity4Pain
Any progress on making that color theory sheet @ShellE?
You never updated us

Capacity4Pain
Hello?
Anyone here?

Marty R
This channel has been really quiet for a long time now.

Capacity4Pain
Yeah, I guess so
It looks like everyone is in the lobby talking about true crime stuff again

Marty R
That's been on a lot of people's minds lately.

Capacity4Pain
Hard not to think about
But it feels too real, you know?
The whole thing is supposed to be about escapism from the real horrors, I thought
Right now the whole server is kinda bumming me out

Marty R
I get that.

Capacity4Pain
I was really hoping the theory channel would be different

Marty R
Different?

Capacity4Pain
More focused I guess
On theories
On the actual comic stuff
Not everything else going on

Marty R
I get that.
Hey @Capacity4Pain.
Do you want to hear my favorite fan theory?

Capacity4Pain
Please
Go for it

Marty R
Have you heard the one where the entire comic is a social experiment?

Capacity4Pain
What sort of social experiment?

Marty R
To see how we react.

Capacity4Pain
I guess anything COULD be a social experiment
It would for sure explain how Langdon was able to get
the PERFECT artist for the job with literally no budget
And pay for hosting costs
Oh, dude, and privatization for the website as well
The whole operation was sort of top tier for a first time
indie project in retrospect, wasn't it?
Holy shit, this is a good one lol

Marty R
Does it make you wonder what they're learning about us
though?

Capacity4Pain
How do you mean?

Marty R
I don't know.
That maybe we're focusing on the wrong part of the comic?
Maybe we're confirming the world's interest in red rooms.

Capacity4Pain
Well, the internet has always had an interest in red
rooms. That's how it caught Langdon's attention in the
first place
There have always been those sort of fucked up stories
about what is going on on the deep web, you know?
So why this?

Marty R
Why this indeed.
It's just something I thought was interesting.
I was scrolling through a bunch of old posts today, the
theories, the comments, even some of the fan art.
I just find it a bit odd how so much of the conversation
focuses on the actual sets and the livestreams and the rooms.

Capacity4Pain
Well they're the focal point of the comic, aren't they?

Marty R
Are they?

Capacity4Pain
Stylistically, they're so bright. So striking

Marty R
Visually, yes.
But when you look at the comic through traditional narrative framing, the sets are little more than exposition. They're war flashbacks.
The focus is definitely supposed to be on the main timeline; on the revenge. That's where the majority of the plot actually takes place.
Hell, Topher is set up as the actual protagonist of Arc 1 and we don't ever talk about him anymore. When was the last time you saw his name mentioned on here?

Capacity4Pain
I guess I never looked at it that way

Marty R
But I'm right.

Capacity4Pain
You're right

Marty R
So what do you think it says about us, then, as fans, as a society, that we only seem to look at the parts that take place inside the red room?

Capacity4Pain
I don't know

Marty R
I think it means we are all a good deal more interested in torture than we like to admit.
Underneath all the character building, and plot, and shine of it, we all just wanted to see the blood.
I think there's something in society that really does need cleansed.

The following text has been taken from the ask blog on Tumblr known as RedAskRed.

 Anonymous asked:

OOC question: Is there a type of RP that you like best?

Well, as someone that is a HUGE fan of the original comic, I obviously like things that are a little dark uwu

The following is taken from The Site.

Welcome back, everyone.

I am sure that some of you are a little curious about my aforementioned side project, and never you mind about that. It shall be revealed to you in due time, when it is finished.

For now, let us focus on the main news about my main project.

The process has started anew.

I am playing it safer this time. Needless to say there will be no actual smithing involved in the process.

I know, I know, the accuracy.

I do not like it any more than you do. Do you know how much it pains me to have to still be bringing you these updates via text? On this shitty plain background no less.

It is not what I wanted when we set out. Perhaps had it not been for my previous slipup, we could have tried a little harder, done a little more.

Because there are developments that you deserve to see, with the new woman.

You would be impressed to know how much she looks like Red, and how easily she has taken to the chains.

I want so badly for you to witness with your own eyes how the chains were forever sealed into place, and shall not be removed until her death.

I want you to see the next stage.

You deserve to believe that she is more than just the first, flimsy practice run.

This will have to be enough for now, because we must all work within our own limitations.

For now, know that it is underway.

Stage 1 went better with this one, much has been learned. Stage 2 is underway, and for now it is just a waiting game while she recovers.

I must rush more than I wanted to, but some parts will still take time.

While I wait, I shall try to get to the bottom of this conundrum I have having with the community of fans right now.

There is much research to be done yet.

—The Creator

The following has been taken from Archive of Our Own.

Violet
BloodyPurpleProse

Chapter 2

The only treatment she had gotten for her cut was the kind she had made herself. She had washed at the wound and bound it with strips of cloth torn from the bottom of her own dress—back when she had been allowed clothes. She had taken care not to pick at the scab, going so far as to bind herself at night when the itching seemed bad enough to drive her to insanity.

It seemed her care had paid off; that and her bravery.

There had only been one position available in the cage, and none could imagine what it might be like. Violet, who even still struggled with the language, had not even known what the word "cage" had meant at the time.

But when she'd registered that they were asking for a volunteer, she had stepped forward without question.

Her reasoning was simple, and so flawed that it would keep her up many nights afterward as she contemplated how stupid and reckless she had been. The logic had been as follows:

They always told the prisoners when something bad was going to be done to them. If they were taking volunteers, then it must be for something different. Different, in her mind at the time, had been synonymous with good.

Even if it haunted her later, how idiotically she had arrived at the conclusion, she had been right to do so.

They'd stripped her down after she'd stepped forward, circling her and appraising her before seeming to deem her worthy of the new life.

She wondered sometimes what had happened to the others. They'd probably thought her mad, or assumed she had given up on life when they had seen her taken away. She doubted any of them could picture what she'd signed up for—just as she could not imagine properly what they were going through now.

Her new life was not perfect.

She was never dressed fully, if at all, and was not even permitted the thin blankets they'd had in the barracks. Often it was too cold her for tastes, but not so frigid that she truly suffered from temperature alone. Instead of being tortured in new ways constantly, or being forced to watch her comrades fall day after day, Violet was permitted a relative life of luxury behind her bars, in full view of the camera, of course.

It was spacious, too, all things considered.

Most of the interior was taken up with the large mattress that made her nights more comfortable, but she had just enough room to pace around the bed on her more restless days.

Recently, she had even been given sheets; a privilege she never tried to abuse by covering herself more than she thought would be permitted.

Sometimes one of the guards would come in and bark orders at her, telling her where to stand or what to do. Sometimes she did not understand these orders, but from the complexity of them, she wondered if her confusion were not part of the point.

What she liked best about the arrangement was that aside from the lack of traditional torture, her time was her own. It was not a good life, perhaps, but it was bearable, and better than she had known for some time. As a girl who had kept her own company all her life, she was easily entertained with nothing but her own mind.

Perhaps if she had not been so lost in her daydreams, she would have seen the woman standing in the doorway, covered in blood.

Notes:

Thank you so much everyone!

I got a lot of really positive feedback on the first chapter of this, and it inspired me to go ahead and post more of what I had written already. That being said, I'm going to be taking a little break from this.

For as nice as everyone has been on here, I have some friends who are not super thrilled with my shift from the fic I was doing to Violet. Apparently there's some weird stuff going on in this community and while everyone I met has been super nice, I understand their concerns.

Thanks for understanding and if any of you are into Mycroft, please check out my long running fic in the meantime.

The following is a private conversation between the famous Mila, and a less famous Michael.

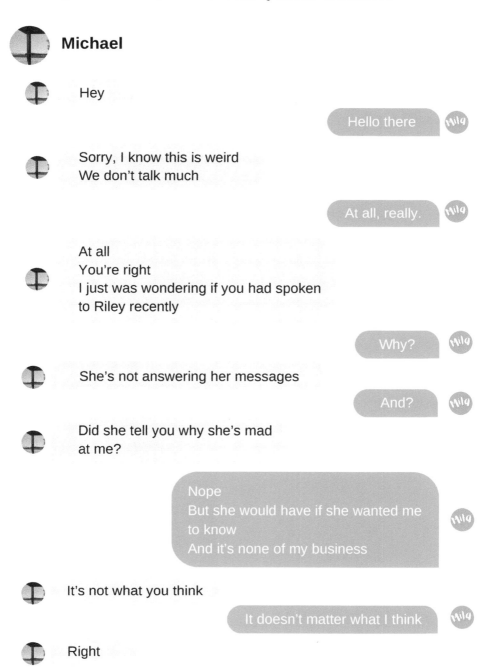

Michael

Hey

Hello there

Sorry, I know this is weird
We don't talk much

At all, really.

At all
You're right
I just was wondering if you had spoken
to Riley recently

Why?

She's not answering her messages

And?

Did she tell you why she's mad
at me?

Nope
But she would have if she wanted me
to know
And it's none of my business

It's not what you think

It doesn't matter what I think

Right

But some advice?
If she doesn't want to talk to you, stop messaging her

Will you just
Make sure she's okay?
She's been upset with me a long time, and I get it
But this isn't like her

I don't want to get in the middle of whatever the hell is going on between you two

Please?
You don't even have to mention me
Just check on her?

--- Today ---

She's fine.

Thank you

This one time
Never again

Understood

New message

The following text has been taken from the ask blog on Tumblr known as RedAskRed.

Anonymous asked:

What makes you think that you have the right to pretend to be Red? There is only one person capable of that, and it's Miss Riley.

I'm sure Riley wouldn't mind. She's an advocate of art in all of its forms, especially when it's pushing boundaries. What pushes boundaries more than interactive fanfiction with original characters thrown in the mix?
Besides, it's a totally common practice on here to RP with existing IPs. It's all in my disclaimer if you check.
~OOC

The following has been taken from Archive of Our Own.

Violet
BloodyPurpleProse

Chapter 3

The woman was thin and had blood streaked across her pale skin. She wore all black, like the guards, but there was not a doubt in Violet's mind that she had once come from the cage, metaphorically if not the literal one in which Violet now resided.

Her manacles fit tight, the chains between them dangled, broken like a sort of demented armor. It made her look stronger than it should have. The links dragging behind her made a scraping sound as she finally stepped into the room.

She looked to the cameras first, counting them. Violet curled up into her pillows, willing herself to be invisible as she watched this strange woman circle the room and count them. Then she began to circle and knocked them down one by one.

She did this with a practiced flick of her wrist, the chain pulling each device to the floor easily from where they had been mounted.

Violet trembled at such disruption, fearing that her luck was about to run out. It did not matter what this woman had once been, a fellow victim, another submissive. Now she was dangerous.

No doubt she wanted something.

Violet shrunk up all the more when the woman approached, tilting her head to one side as she appraised the bars. Then she spoke.

Her voice was deep and flat, with a different accent than the guards. At least it was the same language as Violet had been painstakingly trying to learn. "Did they hurt you?"

Violet shook her head. They hadn't hurt her. Much.

The woman's dark eyes fell to the scar on Violet's chest, and Violet did the one thing she had been trained not to do; she covered herself.

"Can you speak?"

Violet nodded, and then realized her mistake. Her voice, like the rest of her, felt weak, and the foreign word felt awkward in her mouth as she managed to croak out the small "Yes."

"How long have they had you?"

She shrugged. It felt like a lifetime, but also like not enough time for her relative safety to be coming to an end.

"Alright, let's get you out of here."

"Out?"

The woman looked up from where she was already fiddling with the padlock. "You don't want to stay in there, do you?"

Honestly, Violet did not know. Maybe she did.

Notes:

I know it's been a while!

I actually wasn't sure if I'd ever come back to this fic, and I'm sure that the timing must seem really weird with everything else that's been going on lately.

BUT!

I have some exciting news.

I actually can't share it yet, but it involves a certain big creator and this very premise. Let us just say that someone reached out to me about a potential collaboration. Someone you all know. That's all I can say, so please don't ask.

It's hard enough keeping this secret as is, but we all have to wait a little longer.

But it's exciting!

In the meantime, I just wanted to get the ball rolling again. Everyone wish me luck, and hopefully you'll be getting some updates (on the fic and the exciting news) soon.

The following text has been taken from the ask blog on Tumblr known as RedAskRed.

 Anonymous asked:

Common for other IPs and characters, maybe, but Red is special.

I totally agree Anon! If I didn't think Red was special, I would have chosen another character to RP.
~OOC

The following text has been taken from an RP blog on Tumblr known as RedRedRed.

Update: Shutting Down

 blog-redredred

OOC:

It really pains me to say this, but after three years I will be closing down the RP blog.

Earlier this week I said I intended to keep it going, because I felt like we needed the distraction more than ever during Riley's hiatus.

I still believe that, but it's going to have to be a distraction other than the one here.

I was getting some pretty nasty threats.

At first it was just on the ask blog that I set up to accompany this account. A lot of you were asking why I stopped updating with no notice and turned off anonymous asks on there, and honestly it was because I just couldn't handle seeing all of those messages and I didn't want to think about it for a little bit.

Now, unfortunately, they're starting to spill over to this main blog as well, and I just don't need the stress on top of everything else.

I don't want to get into all the specifics. Some of the things have been pretty graphic—including someone who knew my real name and I even got a couple really violent images that really weirded me out. Some real horror movie shit with women who were chained up and burned and oozing and it was just super gross. Some people said really nasty things to me. I was getting a lot of criticism for my RP that I didn't understand Red as a character, or Riley as a creator, and I was "lessening the masterpiece" and like, "not good enough" or whatever.

There have always been a couple weirdos, and I accept that it seems to come with the territory. But lately it's just gotten to be really overwhelming.

The last straw came from when I actually got a really passive aggressive email from someone who I know was personally involved in the creation of the comic, someone who I followed up until very recently.

This isn't a call-out post, I'm not trying to cancel anyone, but if I'm not welcome here I think it's really just time that I leave.

I'll still be online, and those of you who already follow my main know where to find me. For everyone that RP'd with me and asked me questions and just hung out, thank you so much.

This was a really great experience until the end, and I'm glad I did it, even after everything.

I'm sorry it had to end this way.

Bye everyone.

-RRR

The following text is taken from the homepage of MilaStudios.com

This Site Has Been Temporarily Disabled

Dear fans and friends,

It seems that some of my accounts have become compromised. We know that the breach includes my email, Instagram, and LinkedIn, and we're currently trying to see what all has been impacted.

If you have gotten any suspicious emails/messages from someone claiming to be me in the last week or two, I ask that you please reach out—even if it has been verified as coming from my account.

Myself and my team are trying very hard to get to the bottom of this and make sure that the issue is resolved as quickly as possible.

Know that I am deeply sorry for any inconvenience, and especially for any client information that may have been compromised in the breach. Please be assured that all the affected parties have already been contacted, but also reach out if you have any additional concerns regarding your privacy.

Commissions, newsletters, and updates will be temporarily suspended.

I will be resuming my regular content schedule as soon as this is all cleared up and I have the go-ahead from those advising me at this time. They assure me that should be within the week.

I apologize again for any inconvenience this may have caused to you.

Sincerely,
Mila

The following has been taken from The Site, and will conclude Part 2 of this little document. I hate to leave this little research project unfinished, but I must take a page from the book of my hero and go on hiatus after this. One of my most valuable research resources has been cut off, and it seems like a perfect time to return to the goal at hand.

When Riley's transformation has begun, I will return to finish the last two chapters. The fifth, of course, she shall help me write herself.

Hello all,

There is an update of which I feel you should be made aware.

As you know, we have an expedited timeline for this project. It has meant that the streaming has not gone according to plan, which will undoubtedly hurt my profits from this little endeavor.

Needless to say, I was never in it for the money anyway.

I was in it for Riley.

I was in it for the vision.

The glory.

The world, which I believe needs its savior.

Of course, I have the perfect woman in mind to be our Red.

The measures have been put in place to arrange for her arrival into my facility.

The facility, by the way, has been upgraded.

This will not be the interactive live experience that I was hoping for, but one of my tech connections did come through. The next transformation will be recorded in its entirety, and I dare say shall be shareable upon request. We tried to skip to the last stage of the proper Red Room experience, but it makes sense that we needed to try walking before we could run.

You will be a proper audience.

I, soon, will be a proper Creator.

I know the transformation will go smoothly this time. There shall be no more little hiccups like with the Elowen girl.

I know this, because the second test run was very successful.

Perhaps I'll try to get footage of me disposing of this one, just to test out that tech before the final show is ready. There are a couple more things I want to test with her before the end, but it's coming soon.

Those of you following along at home need to start thinking about whether or not seeing the real thing is worth keeping your eyes in your head.

Because Red will be coming for you before you know it.

No one will be safe.

—The Creator

Part 3:
Revenge Arc

IS THIS REALLY WHAT HE THOUGHT WAS GOING TO HAPPEN?

NEWSPAPER

CHAINED BODY IDENTIFIED

The body of a woman in chains washed ashore Saturday evening, and has now been identified as local woman, Elaine Glasgow (23). Glasgow had been reported missing in late March of this year by her distraught mother.

Mrs. Glasgow, the victim's mother, was unavailable for comment, but had reportedly told police several times that her daughter might be wrapped up in some sort of online "cult." The two had been fighting about Elaine's desire to meet up with a boyfriend she had met on the internet through something her mother believes she referred to as "Tor."

Police have not brought any suspects into custody, but the internet history of the deceased girl seems to be a point of interest.

DISCORD, #LOBBY

lobby

InnocentTech
It has to be a copycat, right? The Creator

Olive4
Oh god, not that guy

CreativeNotCreator
What do you mean not that guy?
Like he isn't the greatest villain in contemporary fiction?

Olive4
Oh, that Creator

InnocentTech
What?

Sweetz
Yeah, what?

Olive4
I didn't know you meant the original, sorry

CreativeNotCreator
Who else would we mean?

InnocentTech
Guys, focus. Copycat: yay or nay?

Sweetz
Copycat for sure. I hate to say it, but it looks too similar to be anything but

Ami Gara
I don't know. The reports said she was burned pretty bad, that's not something that was ever in the comic. The chains look the same, but not much else

CreativeNotCreator
That's not true.
In Arc 4 you can clearly see that several of the girls in the back have been burned.

Olive4
I thought you meant that weird edgelord account with all the screen caps of that fake deep web fansite

Sweetz
I mean, I'm sure he didn't burn her because it was or was not in the comics, he did it because he was trying to follow the flashback scene from Arc 5 and it backfired. Burns happen naturally on their own when you try to forge metal around someone in the real world

CreativeNotCreator
What edgelord account?

Ami Gara
No way, guys. No one is smart enough to put together a secret base capable of doing this, but is also dumb enough not to also know that hot metal fucking burns

InnocentTech
That's the part that really trips me up.

Hodeldidit
Hi all!
New to the Discord and the comics, but I do read a lot of true crime. You would be AMAZED at some of the mistakes serial killers get away with when they first get started. A lot of those early kills are really messy.

Sweetz
Well, we're not talking about a serial killer

 Hodeldidit
Not yet.

 Olive4
If he IS a copycat, we won't be talking about a serial killer ever. He'd be keeping them

 CreativeNotCreator
What edgelord account????

 Sweetz
Yeah, that's true

 InnocentTech
Is it? I mean, maybe. But The Creator killed a lot of people. Mostly on stream, but also, there were a lot of bodies in Arc 5 that we just flat out don't know where they came from.

 Sweetz
Maybe it's good we have a true crime person in here for once.
@Hodeldidit would you classify The Creator as a serial killer in the comics?

 Hodeldidit
Yeah, I guess I would. The streams make it almost more of a hitman territory because he's doing it for financial gain, but he has both the body count and timespan to technically be considered a serial killer.

 Olive4
Just a very industrious serial killer

 Hodeldidit
Exactly.

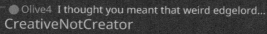 ● Olive4 I thought you meant that weird edgelord...
 CreativeNotCreator
What edgelord account? Please?

 Hodeldidit
Sorry, was I distracting from something?

● CreativeNotCreator What edgelord account? Please?
  Olive4
There's just this account "The Creator" taking screen caps

from some some fake deep web fansite. It was on insta, but I think it got taken down?
I'm sure some of the pics are still floating around somewhere
Basically someone got ahold of a 90s html theme and has been impersonating The Creator on a site, rambling about "what the deep web could be"
Pretending he's going to make the comic real and shit

Hodeldidit
Seriously?

InnocentTech
A little disrespectful, no?

Sweetz
Like you're one to talk lol

InnocentTech
I mean, even for me. With the actual body and everything...

Olive4
I think that's probably why he got busted. Probably thought it was a really funny little side project right up until then

Hodeldidit
Some people are just sick.

CreativeNotCreator
Coming from a true crime fan.

Hodeldidit
What's that supposed to mean?

ModisModding
Hey guys, can you not?
Let's not rehash the true crime fight again
There's enough going on, and I was supposed to be taking a break from this. I've got enough going on offline right now
Could you all just behave for a little while?

CreativeNotCreator
Right, yeah.

REDDIT

r/redcomicmusings · Posted by u/Red Comic Mod

Subreddit Rules and Guidelines

I know that you're all probably tired of the constant reminders from myself and the other mods, but this is important.

What is going on right now is really scary, and it should go without saying that it's not just our community that is shaken up right now. Obviously it is a tough time for the family of the victim as they come to terms with their grief.

The creative team has also been struggling. Between Ms. Langdon's *alleged* disappearance (aka, her hiatus that she announced across multiple platforms and is sticking to) and Mila's accounts being compromised, this feels like a scary and uncertain time in the community.

I know a lot of you are concerned, and that most of that concern is probably coming from a good place—but we all need you to remember that this is not a true crime forum. It is not a conspiracy forum. These are not the end times, and the drama needs to be taken down several notches. This is a fan forum for one specific comic, and I really don't appreciate some of the topics I've seen springing up.

I understand some of you feel the need to talk about what's been going on, but there is a fine line between consoling and fearmongering.

There are some threads that have been left up for support if any of you need it, or would like to offer it. The threads at the top of the forum have been given our express permission to post a couple off topic discussions to keep them contained and easily monitored. Those include a resource thread for ways to support Mrs. Glasgow, a prayer thread for Ms. Langdon, and a scammer reporting thread for Mila. As always, there are links provided in the pinned resource thread where you can donate to either creator and support their various other projects.

There are a lot of really positive ways to come together as a community and send a message to the world that not all fans of this comic are violent and heartless. One of the underlying themes of Red was empathy, and I think we can all embody that together during this time.

What we can NOT do is flood the existing commentary threads, the theories threads, the fan art threads, etc. with speculation, fearmongering, and needless accusations.

We know there has been an influx of people joining the subreddit to troll and stir up drama, and we'll be adding some additional restrictions until this all dies down. What would help us most is if our trusted, established community, would cooperate with us.

Obviously the fact that we were all brought together by this comic does not mean anything other than just that. But there is so much heat and negativity in the fandom right now. The narrative that liking Red makes you a criminal or a sociopath is only furthered by all the infighting that I've seen on here. So it needs to stop.

The most any of us can do right now is not start or engage in any drama here. We don't want to have to boot anyone—especially at this time where we could all use a greater connection to the community—but we will do so if it comes down to it.

If you are warned more than twice, we will not hesitate to ban you. Those of you who have been causing discourse (you know who you are), know that it will not be tolerated moving forward.

Everyone else, we are truly moved to see how active and supportive you have been to the creators who are pushing the boundaries of accessible art to the masses.

As always, thank you.

 Share  Save Hide Report

WATTPAD

 MortaliTea Source Book
by mortalitea

Sources for Current Crimes Episode 32
by mortalitea

In this episode we covered the recent identification of Miss Elaine Glasgow, whose body was found nearly two weeks ago in Elowen, OH.

Included in this episode were facts, clips, quotes and footage that were taken from the following sources:

- Body of a Chained Woman Found (Elowen Daily)
- Chained Body Washes Ashore in Elowen, OH (New York Times)
- Chained Body Identified as Missing Local (Elowen Daily)
- Victim's Mother "Devastated and Appalled" (Elowen Local, Channel 6)
- Comics Are Corrupting Our Youth (OAN)
- The Rise of Violence in Media and in Our Country (Sinclair Broadcast Footage)
- Suspected Creator Goes Missing (New York Times Website)

Additional footage and screenshots were taken from the following locations:

- RileyLangdon.com
- Red Fan Discord Server
- RedComicMusings
- StoptheFilth on TikTok
- InDefenseoftheHorror on YouTube

Thank you so much as always to everyone who watches the videos and clicks through to verify my sources. Affiliate links and sponsors are featured down below.

- Betterhealth/mortalitea
- Shadowsofwar/mortalitea

DISCORD, #LOBBY

lobby

SunnyViolet
@Sweetz I agree. Absolutely sick

CasualObserver
What are we talking about? Couldn't find the start of the convo

 SunnyViolet
Did you hear about MortaliTea?

 CasualObserver
What the fuck is that?

 Sweetz
Some messed up true crime YouTuber thinking to turn a profit off the Glasgow case

 CasualObserver
What?

 PoptartMaster
It's like I was saying though, I don't really see how that's any different from any true crime YouTuber

 Sweetz
Do you seriously not get how it's different?

 PoptartMaster
I get how it's worse, maybe, but different?
Like, it sucks how she's making a video about it RIGHT NOW but also, now is when it's going to get her the most money. I don't get why waiting a year or two is more acceptable when it's going to be made a spectacle of either way

 CasualObserver
I'm still confused

 SunnyViolet
Basically there's a true crime YouTuber who has a series covering current events that is covering the footage surrounding the Glasgow case and the reaction within the comic community.

 Sweetz
With screenshots of inside our server, mind you

 Hodeldidit
Do we have to keep talking about this?

 SunnyViolet
He asked, I'm just trying to explain.

ShellE
I don't get what's so wrong about it
Is it in the best taste? Maybe not
But not talking about it isn't going to bring her back, and
raising awareness is not really any worse than just doing
nothing, which is what most of us can do right now

Sweetz
MortaliTea? Do you seriously not see the issue with that?
She's making the entire field of true crime out to be nothing
but another fucking drama channel
It's sick
She needs to be taken off of YouTube

ShellE
Well that's extreme

Sweetz
Extreme would be saying that she deserves to be the next
victim, if she's going to make light of the whole damn thing
anyway. I think calling for her to be deplatformed is
absolutely reasonable

ShellE
Are you being serious rn?

Olive4
What the fuck?
@ModisModding

Ami Gara
the next victim
?

Sweetz
Yeah, no doubt she's going to make a big video out of that
one too when it finally happens

Ami Gara
Who says there's going to be a next victim?

Sweetz
Killers usually don't stop at 2, do they?

Ami Gara
2?

Sweetz
Glasgow died and now Riley is missing with that freak online

Ami Gara
Be serious

Sweetz
I'm being dead serious

SunnyViolet
You're causing a panic is what you're doing.

ShellE
A moral panic, maybe

 ShellE   A moral panic, maybe

Sweetz
No, ShellE, a real panic. We should all be real panicked right now

PoptartMaster
Why? Even if you're right it doesn't mean that any one of us is in danger

Sweetz
It could mean that one of us is the killer

CasualObserver
Alright, too much for me. I'm tapping out for the day. Hopefully things have calmed down by the time I come back. If anyone wants to play games or something, hit me up

Hodeldidit
What the hell are you talking about?

Sweetz
Think about it. If a fan of Riley's is the one doing all this, why the hell would they not be in the Discord? If it's not here, it's going to be in the Patreon or the Reddit or somewhere because it sure as hell isn't coming out of nowhere

ShellE
You are so full of shit

Sweetz
Am I?

ShellE
Yes. First the true crime community is to blame and needs to be stopped, and now you're actually accusing people in the server of kidnapping Riley? Some of us have been around here for years. I hope you get banned

Sweetz
Yeah, I'm the one that's going to get banned. I've been here longer than you, dickhead. If anyone would be for defending these victims it would be Riley, and you know it.

ShellE
If anyone would NOT be calling for the deplatforming of creators, it would be Riley. Fucking threats were being made against her life before she went missing and she didn't ask for censorship then. She wouldn't now. And she wouldn't give a fuck if an established news channel online decided to cover news

Sweetz
She would care if people are losing their lives! She knows that's not something to make light of. What do you think the whole damn comic was about in the first place?

ShellE
Okay, there's a huge difference between making videos online and being in support of people's lives being taken. Are you a big enough idiot that I seriously have to explain that to you? You can condone free speech and fair use without having to condone serial killers.

HHMarch
He's not a serial killer

Sweetz
What?

ShellE
Seriously? Not the point, dude

HHMarch
Not the point, but it is important. You guys are talking about the next victims and serial killers and pointing fingers, but he's not a serial killer. If you believe the guy that took her was that guy who was making threats, then you know that he's not going to kill Riley.

Olive4
Okay, can we all just admit how fucking creepy it is that we're having this conversation? We came here because we like a comic and now we're practically taking bets on whether the creator of it is going to live or die
@ModisModding what the fuck?
Where are you?

Sweetz
Stop trying to report us to Mod
He's not here

 ShellE
This whole place is going to shit

 HHMarch
It's not a bet. He told us exactly what he's going to do
He's going to turn her into Red

 Sweetz
That's so fucked up

 HHMarch
It's what HE said
I'm just reminding everyone
He went into some pretty explicit detail on his blog. His
plan is to kidnap Riley because he thinks she's created
something that needs to be brought into our reality.
He's going to chain her up and if he doesn't kill her on
accident like he did with the last one, then he's going to let
her escape so she can have the revenge arc she always
dreamed of

 Sweetz
That SHE dreamed of?! Are you fucking kidding me?

 HHMarch
I'm not saying that I agree with him
I'm just saying she wrote the blueprint for what he's
trying to do
Death isn't involved

 PoptartMaster
I mean, he's got a point

 Sweetz
DOES HE?

 PoptartMaster
Again, I'm not saying that it's right. But it's not like we're
dealing with a serial killer. I don't think he'd kill Riley and
right now, maybe that's something to hope for

 Sweetz
Wtf
I can't even
I can't

PoptartMaster
I mean
Come on
You know I didn't mean it that way
Obviously I'm not hoping for that. I hope she's safe and
just like, in witness protection or whatever.
But it would be better than her being taken by an actual
serial killer

Sweetz
HE HAS KILLED ONE WOMAN ALREADY
How is this fucking better??

PoptartMaster
Because @HHMarch is right, he won't kill her
If he's planning to recreate the comic then he's going to give
her the opportunity to escape. When she does it's not like
she's going to help him recreate her comics by going on a
killing spree and picking off the men who watched her get
tortured—they don't exist
She's going to go to the police, and help put him behind bars

Sweetz
After she gets tortured, you mean.

PoptartMaster
But no one else would die, which is the point

Sweetz
No, the point is that this is a real person
A real, flesh and blood, missing person that we've all been
idolizing for years. I don't understand how this is the
conversation we're having about her right now

HHMarch
It's a fucked up world we're living in right now. But it
doesn't do anyone good to be wrong

ShellE
And it doesn't hurt anyone to be made aware of the
situation, either. Even if you don't like it, or the tone of the
people who are covering it.

Sweetz
I can't rn
I just can't

Damsel No More Website Review

Damsel

NO MORE

Product: Damsel No More Hot Pink Pocket Keychain Taser Cute Clip-On For Real Protection
User: RileySaysFU

★☆☆☆☆

Does your page share the bad reviews?

Seriously, where do you put them? I was scrolling through the site and I only saw positive comments. 'This mace is so cute and discreet! I feel safer already!' Bullshit.

There is no way that THIS many people got suckered into your weird pyramid scheme, bought all your #girlboss products, and were actually happy with the result.

For context:

I did not, nor would I ever, purchase from your company. My mother is a serial MLM victim and even though she and I have not spoken face to face since I was in high school, she got it in her head that what I needed to protect myself in the big city that I've been living in alone for nearly a decade was this pink, plastic piece of garbage.

It's ugly. It's not subtle. It looks cheap. AND IT DOESN'T EVEN WORK!

Do the all caps help? Do you potentially find them jarring? So do I. So stop sending me emails that open with 'HEY GIRL' and finish with you begging me to shill this shit for you. I'm not interested. I work as a writer and would be willing to bet all $15 of my life savings that I'm in a better financial position than 90% of your "company."

If you are a person reading this who is thinking about buying this product for actual self-defense reasons, DO NOT. If you a person reading this who is thinking about buying ANYTHING from them, don't. You can get these tasers and mace and your cute little magenta brass knuckle keychains from Amazon for half the price. They're a better quality and I just feel like I should mention this again, not hot pink. Unless you are literally Barbie and everything you own is already this color, hot pink plastic draws a hell of a lot more attention than black or silver. It just does.

If you are a person who is combing through these comments to bury the negative ones, if you are a salesperson in this company, if god forbid this is YOUR website: get out. Get out now.

I am seriously worried for the financial and mental well-being of anyone who is involved with this scam. This product is trash, it endangers the lives of women who think this will actually save them in an emergency, and you're probably paying for the 'privilege' of selling it.

Take this as your sign or whatever to get the fuck out of this mess and save as many people as you can before the door hits your ass.

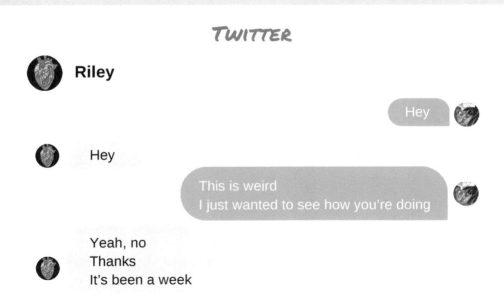

TWITTER

Riley

Hey

Hey

This is weird
I just wanted to see how you're doing

Yeah, no
Thanks
It's been a week

Is now a bad time?

It's always a bad time lately
But we can talk
I'm just trying not to obsess over it,
you know?

You mean the news?

Yeah, the news

That makes sense

Yeah
How are you handling everything?

It's been a transition recently

Right, some heavy stuff

It feels like we're really coming to the
end of something big
You know?

It's weird
But it does kind of feel that way

Can I ask you something?

Anything

Do you ever think about Red?

Hard not to these days

But before they found the girl
Did you still think about Red?

All the time
That comic was how I got discovered

I could never forget about it
Even if I tried

Do you wish you could?

Yes
No
Maybe
Sometimes, this last week I guess

I get that

What about you?
Do you wish you could forget?
Do you regret saying yes?

Oh Riley
I never said yes
This was just something I was born
to do
That you and I were meant to do
together

It felt like that for a while, didn't it?

But you don't think so anymore?

I don't know anymore
Everything feels so wrong

Right

You know this isn't your fault, right?

I know
But it's good to hear
Riley?

Yes?

Do you regret the ending?

What?

Of the comic?
Do you like how it ended?

Yes?
That's how it was supposed to end
Don't you think?

I don't know
No

What would you have changed?

I know the audience didn't need
the answers
But I think Red deserved them

She didn't want them

I guess that's the part I
disagree with

Why?
She'd heard him talk so much

Way too much
He never shut up
But if I were Red
And I had been hurt
Chained
Touched
It would not be enough for me
that the person responsible was
just dead.
Just like that
I'd want the person who thought

> up all those tortures to feel them
> To answer for them

She'd had her fill of torture by
the end

> Don't you think she'd have
> questions?

Maybe
But I think she was just ready to
be done

> I'm not ready to be done

What?

> I have questions, Riley
> For my creator

What do you mean?

> I want to know why

Mila?

> Why did you create me?
> Why did you think those awful
> things?

Mila, what the fuck?

> He's dead, Riley
> But he didn't think this up
> You did

Who is this?

> You and I, Riley
> We can change the ending.

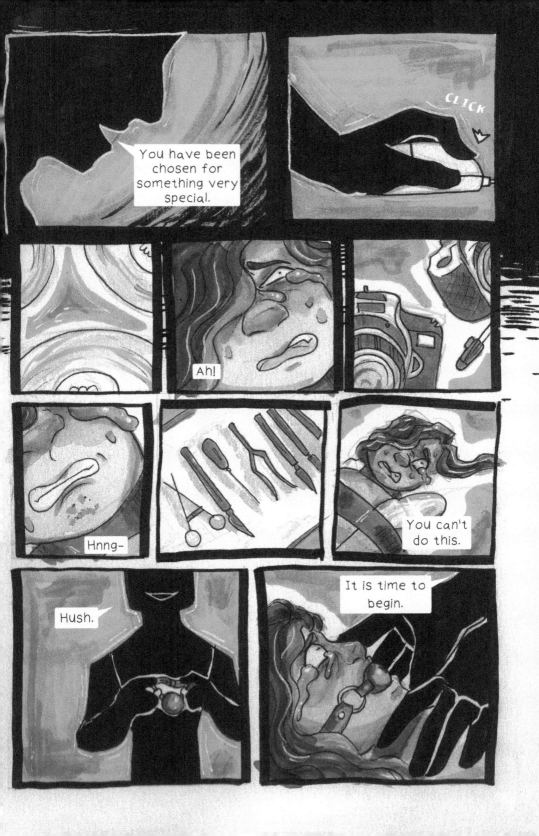

PART 4
HEART-EATER

WHAT WILL BECOME OF HER?

There is a very interesting collection of movies. Not adult movies, like you were hoping to find, but a lot of the NC17 kind. The horror stuff you would have needed an ID to see in theater—at least for the ones that made it into theaters. Some of them look too bloody for even that, if you had to guess.

You don't know. You were never into horror before recently.

And all the rooms are sort of like this. There are no condoms under the bathroom sink, no razors, little enough makeup. The living room, such as it is, has been turned into a gloomy sort of home office. You can't imagine working here, though, with all the sounds of traffic and sirens and shouting coming from outside. It's not a great area.

The kitchen is a five-foot square with a fridge and cabinets that are all empty, save for a couple off-brand energy drinks. You crack one open but leave it unfinished because it tastes like shit.

You hear them coming up the stairs and you ready yourself for the fight of your life.

They're stronger than you, but not as strong as you'd expected. You have the element of surprise. You have the syringe.

All they have is a pink taser and you happen to know already that it doesn't work.

By the time you get the body in the car and bound tightly, you're starting to wonder if it was all too easy, or if it was perhaps a waste of your time, your freedom.

You go back upstairs one more time just to lock up and grab a change of clothes. There's nothing nice. It's not like you were expecting formalwear, but you aren't too keen on the ratty jeans and black T-shirts bearing the posters of these disturbing ass horror movies. The wardrobe is as bland and depressing as everything else.

Then you find the envelope.

You know that it's special because you find it hidden inside a shoebox.

It's one of the big manila kind, and there's a print taped to the front of it. It's black, with a red frame, and an illustration of what appears to be a pair of lips sucking up a human heart like spaghetti.

Your victim is in the trunk already and you don't know how much you dosed them with or how long it will last. So you don't have time to go through the interesting find at present—but at least you know you got something interesting, in case this whole revenge thing turns out to be a bust.

So you change as quickly as you can, and then you start driving. They don't even scream when they wake up, and you start to feel almost guilty for what you've been planning on doing to them.

It's been one of those days for me.

Anyway, Riley Langdon is here, and I haven't decided yet if I'm going to kill her or not.

Inspiration/Brainstorming

• LolitaMaker

I want to scrap the underage portion of this. Aside from the fact that her age will never be explicitly stated, Red herself should look like a young but ADULT woman (early twenties, maybe). The terror shouldn't come from the idea that this could happen to kids, but rather the idea that it could happen at all.

I do want to draw some inspiration from it, though, since it's one of the most famous deep web legends and even though it's not technically a red room, there's some crossover.

- Financially motivated villain • Body modding
- Heavy bondage • Sexual component

• A Girl I used to know

I want to scrap the recurring nature of this one, but I like the personal connection, drawing the viewer in. Topher definitely shouldn't know Red, as it takes away from her mystique, but perhaps she reminds him of someone else.

Opens up a question of complacency with Topher, as well — would he have gotten involved or tried to help if she had looked some other way? These could be the sorts of things he's wrestling with already before she kills him.)

✱ Also like the "pleasureable" aspect of the streams →

→ adding to the discomfort of the audience. Will probably want to work some standard fetish gear into the background of the sets so that the implication can be made without the comic itself ever crossing into erotica.

- **The Game Starts Here**

Hate to admit it, but Reddit guy was right. This is a much creepier and more satisfying deep web experience than the real thing.

- **One Thing About Tor**

This is the fictional deep web I want Red featured on.

- Bitcoin converters   - Trackers
- Hackers   - Illicit chats
- Video embedding   - Livestreams
- Hitmen

And of course, the classic invitation to the

(red room)

Amazing, isn't it?

It starts with these derivative little napkin notes and suddenly there are people willing to kill over this creation.

She didn't even think of anything new from the looks of it, she just wove all her favorite bits together into a nightmare that actual women were then forced to live. Some hero, huh?

I think if I could do it all over again and be anything, it would probably be a writer.

This woman writes about blood and chains and now look at her. Well, maybe not where she's at right now.

But how she's cherished. How she's talked about.

The chosen one.

A savior.

The Real Red.

Those were all things that the man said of the Great Riley Langdon when he was torturing me.

The sick thing—well, a sick thing—is that I think he wanted me to be more impressed by this fictional character, like he didn't even realize how he spoke about the writer.

Maybe if I hadn't been a practice run, and he had tried harder to mold me properly, things would have been different.

Maybe then I would have wanted to just kill her, clean and simple like Red does for her creator in the comic.

But that's too easy, isn't it?

Now that I have seen for myself how powerful it is to be a storyteller, I need to think about the next part very carefully.

I need to think about which stories get told.

The Creator's website, for instance, does not deserve the update that he is dead. He failed to bring about a legacy, and deserves to be left to oblivion. Likely he will be viewed as a fraud, or an anonymous shadow, and either is fine with me.

But I do keep coming back to finish this little project of his.

It's private.

Just mine and his. And he won't get the benefit of it anymore, which makes it essentially just mine.

I want to see how it ends.

I'm just dying to know what happens to our dear protagonist.

FROM THE FOLDER

Thursday
6/13/13
I did it.

I finally fucking did it.

I got home from work today to find mom burning all my notebooks in the backyard. The journals, it seemed, were already nothing but ash. I tried to salvage what odd pages I could. I screamed and asked what the fuck she was doing.

The way she tells it, she was cleaning my room when my journal fell open onto a page where I happened to have called her "stupid" for falling into another pyramid scheme.

I believe exactly 0% of that story.

My mother never cleans unless it's for a presentation, and the house looked like shit except for my room, which she had obviously just trashed. I'm guessing she probably needed another couple hundred bucks to keep her makeup selling status, and since her account is drained, she went poking around in my things for some of my fry money. If I hadn't been saving, I doubt she'd have cared about me enough to snoop.

I don't even really believe the part about her being stupid. I wish she were stupid, because that's something that could be fixed. That would make it less her fault. She could learn. I think she's stubborn, and that's a lot worse. She's selfish, and she's so obsessed with finding an easy out of the life dad left her that she hasn't let herself realize that she's paying money to do other women's makeovers, and losing money all along the way the last ten years.

Over half my life, she's cared more about this absurd string of businesses than about me, her own flesh and blood.

I've known that. That doesn't hurt half so bad as the loss of my stories.

I'm not going to pretend there was any award-winning fiction in there. But they were my words. My escape. I didn't realize until that moment she had any new ways of hurting me, but she did.

It made the decision a hell of a lot easier when she tried to follow up the bullshit with an ultimatum. She told me I could buy-in to work for her, or I could start paying rent.

I chose firmly to do neither.

I could have yelled at her, or explained how the fast food job had made more money a week than her entire year's worth of makeup sales. I could have tried to go over the math with her again. Hell, I had enough cash on me at the moment to toss rent in her face just to prove a point.

But I decided that I was done trying to prove anything to her.

She screamed and shouted at me while I was packing my things. She said I'll be back, that I'll never make it in the world without her, that I have nowhere to go. She told me not to come crawling back when I run out of my money. It was obvious she never thought I'd go, that she didn't realize I've had arrangements made for this moment for months.

I might well run out of money, but I sure as hell am not stepping foot onto that property again. Not ever. I would sooner die.

Being out is the best thing that has happened to me in a long time.

Some things that don't feel great?

My car is making a weird sound, and might not get me another 14 hours into the city.

This hotel costs a lot more than I thought it would.

I met Michael online, so he might well be catfishing me, or he could be a creep or a serial killer, or all of the above.

But those are problems for tomorrow.

Tonight, I just feel so fucking free.

It is much more intimate to be going through these hand-written words than it was to just be following the conversation online. I wish I hadn't lost her phone.

Left her laptop.

I imagine there would be treasure troves of personal information on there. Notes to herself. Story ideas?

I am lucky to have found this, though. This envelope has the good things, the private things. Relics of a history far more vulnerable than the one told to me by the woman in the other room.

You know she told me under duress, in pain, under threat of death, that she has no parents? She said she never knew her father and her mother disowned her?

Technically, maybe, but how I'd long to have a fight like the one she described with her mother in those pages? Something so easy to fix. So tangible.

It seems clear to me that Riley, were she not so stubborn, could walk right back into this woman's life. For the price of what? Pride? A makeover?

It's amazing what some people will take for granted.
Still, I do wonder what was in those notebooks that were lost.
What horrors lurked with in.

What other torments someone—I—might have suffered had they been birthed into the world instead of burned.

Maybe I understand, just a little, why she's mad.

CROWLEY
Literary Agency

Dear Ms. Langdon,

Thank you so much for submitting your manuscript to me. Unfortunately, after careful consideration, I have decided that it is not a great fit for my services at this time.

To be honest, I was surprised by the graphic nature of your piece. One of the reasons it took me so long to send a response is because I truly could not get some of the imagery out of my head. Those are usually the stories that I prefer to represent, but I just don't know of any markets that are open to something so extreme.

I don't know how long you have been submitting this to agents, but I hope this rejection does not discourage you too greatly. Your writing is imaginative, and has a certain cinematic flair that I think is going to be a great asset.

I wish you all the best in finding a home for this book, and would like to invite you to submit to me again. If you ever have a piece that is less brutal, I hope that you'll consider sending it my way.

Sincerely,
Amanda Crowley

CROWLEY
Literary Agency

2015 Submission Tracker

Heart-Eater
Not sure about all of this one, but it seems important

—Amanda Crowley— REJECTED
—Mary Zenon — REJECTED
— Pickman's Literary Journal — REJECTED
— Cemetery Dr. Media — REJECTED
—Horror House — REJECTED

A Mountain in Heels
—Bones by the Dozen— REJECTED

Proxy
—Bring Me the Living Zine — REJECTED
— Undead, Zombies, and the Reanimated— REJECTED

Just Like Her
—Bathory Review —PENDING

Bruises
—Blood and Lace — ACCEPTED

Sunday
2/22/15

I haven't written anything longhand in a while, but this just doesn't feel real to me yet, and I don't think typing it out was doing it for me.

I found a comic artist for Red.

I found the comic artist for Red.

A couple people had sent me some reference sketches, and there was some other, vague, polite interest. No one professional at first, no one with comic experience, or who I thought had a decent chance of sticking with it until the end.

To be honest, I cared more about that than the style.

The other side of that coin was the people who were too professional, people who would expect to be paid per page.

I believe that artists deserve to be paid for their work, and as a writer that has ONLY ever been paid in exposure, I know what bullshit that is. But I really just don't have the money to pay per page for an entire comic's worth of content. I know I can be verbose in my storytelling, it may well take a couple years to finish. If we also had to wait for me to save up per page... it would never get done.

Just as I was looking over price lists and preparing myself to abandon the mission, I got a private message from Mila.

Mila.

The Mila.

I've been following their work for a couple months on Tumblr, and they're absolutely amazing. I was surprised at the interest from them, not just because they're higher-profile than me as a creator, but also because their work is far more surreal than what my comic proposes.

That was something they brought up with me, however, during our back and forth. They've apparently been looking for a project they believe will challenge them. "A different kind of horror," they said.

I have never been so proud to have my work described as different.

The best part is that they are looking at this more as a collaboration. They like that I have the main story beats down from start to finish (neither of us wants this to last forever) but that I am not attached to all of the design elements as of yet.

Working on it together instead of delivering orders to be completed makes me feel a lot better about them putting in the work for essentially nothing but credit. Of course I did offer to pay for the hosting costs for the site.

As to how I'm going to swing that, I don't know yet. The budget is already pretty tight right now, but I'll make it work.

I've got an artist on board now, a good artist.

And I can't explain it.

This project feels different than the others.

2016 Submission Tracking

Heart-Eater
- Horror House – REJECTED
- Shadow Lit Press – REJECTED
- Yellowstone Media – REJECTED

Proxy
- Haunted and Wandering – REJECTED

Virtual Ghost Town
- Phantasmographic – PENDING

Fuzzy Logic
- Viral Attitude Zine – REJECTED

Our Funeral
- Non-Standard Scripts – REJECTED

Questionable Erotic Content
- Pulptastic Zine – ACCEPTED

IS THIS ALL THE HARDER SHE TRIED?
WAS SHE SO DISCOURAGED?

When the man was torturing me, it seemed to go on forever. I was barely left alone long enough to catch my breath, let alone try to fall asleep to the 'clink clink clink' of those stupid manacles.

It's different from the other side of it.

It seems like all I do now is wait.

Of course, I don't have the practice that he got. No trial victims for me. I didn't have a "volunteer" to let me have any practice swings, or who I could accidentally kill as a freebie.

He told me that was what happened to his last Red. He said he experimented on her, and she'd gotten burned, and that those burns had gotten infected, and they had festered. He said she had suffered a lot at the end. He told me he'd have let her suffer for the cameras if he could have gotten the streams up and running beforehand, just so people could see how long it would have taken.

But he didn't have that kind of patience, and in this one regard, I can't say that I blamed him.

That's why he got me, apparently. Because the first one had died too soon.

The chaining went a lot better for me, he said, and would probably be the very same set that "the real Red" would get to wear once I was out of them.

While he had me anyway, while everything else was set in motion, he said it wouldn't hurt him to practice.

I would lie there on the table, bleeding, sobbing, and I would wonder how exactly someone would need so much practice with these tools of torture. He'd slice me deeply, every time, and I screamed every time, and I did not ever understand.

It's a dance. You have to know your partner.

If I cut her too deep, it draws pain from the other locations that I want to hurt, from the bruising around her chains, from the sting of her piercings.

If I push her too hard, I will need to wait for her to recover, or else she won't feel all of what I mean to do next.

The waiting takes a long time when you're the one who doesn't need a break.

Luckily, I suppose, I have this little side project.

And company.

Monday
9/18/17

I am beginning to wonder if I have made it.   DOES SHE HAVE
       TO ASK THIS? DOES SHE FEEL LIKE SHE'S MADE IT NOW?
Obviously I haven't made it big. I'm not set for life, I'm not a household
name, and honestly I don't even know what other measures of big
success are supposed to be for someone in the entertainment industry.

I guess it would be nice to quit the day job. But I'm no longer supplementing
the income from the day job with odd data entry hours, and that feels huge.

For me, success as a writer has always meant getting to write what I want.
I guess long term, my biggest goal is a modicum of financial stability from
getting to write full time. I may still be a long way off from that, but I'm
beginning to realize that there are actually some degrees of success worthy
of celebration before the final stage.

The comic has taken off.

Again, it's not bringing in a lot of money, but I'm breaking even on hosting
costs and Mila and I are seriously talking about merchandizing. I remember
when we put up the first few pages how having merch felt like such a pipe
dream but now it's feasible - practical, I dare say, with all the attention
that it's gotten lately.

Even when I found out just how long it was going to take to do all
5 full-color arcs, I couldn't imagine myself taking on any projects but Red
until it was done. And now...

Gut Reactions was just me fucking around, killing some time. I didn't
think of it as a side project, let alone something that would, or even
could take off as well. But it seems to be doing some numbers.

If I spent the money I had been using to host Red taking a bit of a gamble on my Word Press site, upgrading the plan to support advertisers...

It isn't entirely impossible that by the end of the year I could be looking at two small, but steady streams of income that are just from my writing. This, without the constant grind and failure of querying my novel and my weird little short stories that no one seems to want to read.

Maybe that failure is why I feel so much like an imposter lately — even with all these small successes coming my way?

In my head, before today, before I started to really think about it, I had always seen success equating to a book deal, to publications, to my name in print.

Maybe that just wasn't the path for me?

It's weird to see these other, non-book projects begin to flourish — to the point I don't even remember the last time I subbed for anything. It's not that I'm less passionate about these new things, because I'm not. I love doing Red. I love doing Gut Reactions. They're just not what I always pictured myself doing.

Maybe it's okay to see where this path leads, though.

Tuesday
5/14/19

Michael left ~~today~~.

I can't believe he would actually do this to me.

We had talked about it, and I knew it was coming, but it still feels like a betrayal. He knows that I didn't want him to go, and he went anyway.

The worst part was how patronizing he was about the whole thing. He said he was doing it for me, because I had gotten to a point in my life where I didn't need him around anymore. He's leaving and throwing himself a little pity party on the way out because he apparently knows "what I need."

Unbelievable.

Maybe he gets to be a little patronizing because he rescued me once, forever ago, when I really needed a place to go. He took a chance on some eighteen-year-old online that he'd only known for a couple months. Is that how he saw us this whole time? **HE WAS STILL CHECKING UP ON HER TWO BEDROOMS. DOES SHE REALLY NOT SEE IT?**

I thought he was my friend.

My close friend.

My only friend.

And he's apparently just thought of me as someone whose mess he's been cleaning up for the last six years.

But I helped him, too, even if he doesn't want to admit it.

I know he could have afforded to live here without me, but I paid my share.

I burned through all my high school savings to give him rent in advance so he could trust me, and I worked my ass off so I wasn't late a single time pitching in.

I wonder how easy it would been to save for his nicer, two-bedroom if I hadn't been pulling my damn weight from day one.

For him to have the nerve to tell me that I deserve my own bedroom, that I'm doing "too well" to be sleeping on the pull-out still, just because I had one viral moment. It's not like any of that attention has been good. It's not like producers are lining up to work with me.

I told him. I fucking told him, and do you know what he said to me? He said he'd help me with rent if I needed it.

Like somehow I'm both too big a name for him to be associating with, and also somehow his fucking charity case?

I just can't wrap my head around it.

I told him that if he was going to go not to even worry about it and just get the hell out. He looked hurt. Like I'm the one who is changing everything? Like I'm the one leaving? Like this is somehow my fault?

Maybe I should be grateful he did this before I quit my shitty day job.

Mostly I'm just pissed.

At Michael, yes, but also at myself for not ever taking the time to make other friends in the city. Maybe not making other friends at all.

Last month I was just so excited to finally have some savings started and this month somehow I'm a hermit with no furniture, trying to forget that anyone else ever lived here.

I just can't wait for things to feel easy.

When the hell does that start?.

I guess I was wrong, there was a man in her apartment once.

For six years, apparently.

It is interesting to me how these little snippets of her life paint such a different picture of her than the story that the bleeding woman behind me seems to tell about herself.

I've learned a lot about her through our conversations that I don't think anyone else knows.

I've learned a lot about her through these pages that I don't think even she herself knows.

Maybe it's because I built her up in my head for so long, but reading through the best pieces of her life, the worst pieces, I can see through all the words and nonsense and insecurities into the version of Riley Langdon that never was.

I entertained the notion of trying to create her.

After all, I was powerful enough to be Red for a time, I escaped, I killed him. Why could I not be the next iteration of The Creator?

Why could I not make something truly wonderful out of this mess of a woman who is already so well loved?

I could.

I am of the belief that I could do anything I wanted. But as much as the idea interests me on paper, it's something I don't really want to follow through on.

Molding her into something new, let alone something better, would take a long time. It would take a lot of training and patience—and for what? For the chance that she still resents me? Kills me? Turns me in?

It's not worth it.

I'm starting to finally understand the end of her comic, why Red kills quickly at the end of the arc.

As my anger turns to pity for her, I realize that I too am losing my appetite for vengeance.

For blood.

Whatever I end up doing with her, I think I'm going to want to be wrapping it up soon.

FROM THE ENVELOPE

Dear Ms. Langdon,

The studio has decided not to pick up your treatment. While we think the work was very good, we were hoping for something a bit more cutting-edge.

We are all fans of your previous film, and the director we have on board hopes that he gets the chance to work with you at some point on a future project. We just felt like you played it too safe with the script that you sent in.

If you have any more ideas, we would be happy to read more from you at any time.

Best Regards,
J.H. Stewart

Acquisitions Manager at Darkline Studios

Dear Ms. Langdon,

On behalf of ComicVerse Conventions, we would just like to sincerely apologize. We understand that you got into an altercation during one of our panels and that our security staff was not able to properly assist you before the point of escalation.

While we take full responsibility for our part in the incident, we cannot condone violence or threats of any kind.

Though you said in your statement with security you felt as though your fellow panelist was being threatened after a guest made certain offensive (aggressive, in your own words) comments regarding gender, we do not feel as though we have the adequate means to make sure that the environments in upcoming panels are more secured. In light of that, we think it would be best if you did not finish your tour with our events this summer.

We thank you sincerely for the work you have already done with us this convention season, but we will be suspending your contract moving forward.

Your co-panelist, Mila, has already voluntarily withdrawn as they were somewhat shaken by the event.

We hope that you understand our position, and that we have the opportunity to host you under different, safer circumstances where you do not feel that yourself or your colleagues are being threatened.

If there is anything else we can do to ease this shift in plans, we hope that you will feel comfortable reaching out.

Cordially, *I guess this is why she doesn't do more conventions.*
The ComicVerse Convention Team

I used to envy her.

Not that she'd be the one to kill him, an honor I eventually claimed for myself, despite all he had told me.

But I envied her for the way he loved her. The way he spoke about her. The way he planned from the very first day that she was worthy of life, and I was worthy of practice, so that she could live. He was even planning to die for her.

No one has ever felt that way about me.

Even when he was inside me, he only saw her, was only thinking about Riley.

Or about Red.

Or about how fucking perfect Riley would be if he could turn her into this more perfect, fictional version of herself.

I don't even think he really saw me as I was killing him. Not truly. He didn't register that it wasn't his Red, that it was me.

And why should he?

I've been thinking of myself as Red too, for some time now, if I'm being honest. This better, fictional version of myself that can survive anything. That can get revenge for all the pain.

Pain she caused.

She gets to go out and play champion to the battered women of the world, but I don't think she gives a damn about us. Not really. How did she think we would feel reading her words? Her sick fucking comic.

It takes the attention away from us and puts it back on her.

The main fucking character, who people must be talking about always. Even when I am being brutalized and nearly murdered, it was her name on his tongue. She is all anyone can ever think about.

And I hate her for it.

I really do.

I think she deserves to go through what I've been through. I think if she wants to be free, she can go ahead and earn it like I did.

But there are moments. Just, these little moments, when we talk, and I can see a little bit of what everyone else sees in her. Her cooperation with me, in rare instances, feels like she's opening up, and not like she's scared for her life. They feel all the more special because I know she's a private person.

When I'm reading about her, when I'm working on finishing this document that was dedicated to her, I get so frustrated. She's been given so many opportunities that she's been blind to.

She finished a whole damn book! And those short stories! She has a comic and a movie and a website and people paying her because she's creative, and talented, and she wants to throw it all away. She gave up. She stopped sending stories. I wouldn't do that if I could write. If I had these ideas. If a movie studio, a fucking movie studio, told me to send in another script? Well fuck, I'd do it.

She's strong, too.

I know she's independent and stubborn, but when I poked her with that needle to get her here, she just let me. She didn't even try to escape.

She's so bitter and angry and I honestly think maybe she wants this. Maybe she wants to die. And I read her words and how she interprets all these fortunes, and I think maybe this is just another chance that she's ready to throw away.

And I want to kill her.

Then, like I said, there are these times when I get so mad, and I ask her for clarification.

And sometimes she just says something that will make me

understand better why she is so beloved.

Sometimes she tells me things that are too beautiful to be committed to paper.

It feels almost like she's fighting for me, instead of against me.

I love her.

And I want her dead more than ever.

Dear Miss Langdon,

We are sorry to extend this invitation to you without further advance notice, but we would love to give you a panel room at this year's AkaCon.

We were so disappointed you weren't able to make it last year, and we've had a few last-minute cancellations.

We understand if a week's notice simply isn't enough time to prepare, but your stay at the convention center would be comped, and we would love to have you.

There are already a couple of Red fan panels scheduled over the weekend, and we think a lot of fans would be pleased to see you.

We hope that you'll consider the offer, and that you'll let us know ASAP.

—The Whole Team
(AkaCon Official Members)

Friday
(?)

I haven't been sleeping right since I started my hiatus.

I lie awake wondering if the whole thing has blown over. If it's gotten worse. I wonder if I'll even know when it's time to come back online. If I should go back at all.

It's been a few days, at least, since I've called it. There was this immense freedom when I turned my computer off, like I might be done with it all forever. Not just the computer itself, but all the rest of it too.

The Patreon. The updates. The communities. The fighting.

Everything.

I have lived for these projects and nothing else for so long that I was starting to forget there was anything else. Did my idea of fulfillment change somewhere along the way? Or am I just burnt the fuck out?

I used to journal.

I remember all my journals got destroyed and I quit. But it was like a smoker quits, you know, and sometimes I used to still write out the important stuff on loose leaf paper when I got really stressed or excited. When I needed a fix. I kept the pages in my folder.

It was one of those cheap, cardboard folders that I've been reusing for stuff since about the 8th grade, and I don't even know how it made the trip out here with me. It was probably in my backpack when I tossed all my stuff in my car.

I remember being oddly sad about it when the side gave out and I finally needed to replace the damn thing. Only it was like my journal, where I never really replaced it properly. I shoved all the papers that I'd been saving inside this big envelope that had contained the one print copy of my piece of shit manuscript.

I feel sort of like that envelope right now.

I'm just a pile of angry thoughts and rejections shoved in around the book no one ever wanted to read.

Red was supposed to be phase one in my plan. It was supposed to be me dipping my toes into the pool of the self-publishing world. I was going to get a reader base and start seeing if I could publish something extreme on my own without anyone's help.

What happened to all that?

I guess maybe I thought the stories were too similar? Red was too much like the protagonist of my novel, Liv—angry, and the revenge thing, and at the time the setting didn't seem like a big enough difference.

Not that it would have mattered, I guess. Red was an integral part either way, and that was the part that ended up being the problem.

I don't even know if I believe that it is a problem.

It seems outlandish to me. Narcissistic even, to believe that I am the sort of creator who would have other people die over their creations.

Just because I live online in an echo chamber where I hear about my work all the time, doesn't mean that I actually have influence. It doesn't mean much of anything.

I don't believe Elaine Glasgow died because of anything I wrote.

So why the guilt?

Maybe it's just that anger I've lived with all my life—the anger that the problem is bigger than me, out of my control. If some crazy fan actually had done it, I would have the power in that situation, wouldn't I? I could denounce them, I could protect any future victims, I could bring about some kind of justice. There would be things for me to do, and I'd matter.

Fuck, that's a sick thing to think about, huh? That I would matter more if the killer had read my comic?

But also, wouldn't it be true?

I think society would treat me better, if they saw that my words had that kind of impact. I think they'd treat anyone better who had that kind of influence.

I think I feel guilty because a part of me wishes I were responsible.

I really need to buy a new journal. A real one.

There are some thoughts that are just a little too fucked for the internet.

I went ahead and read the last item in the folder, the novel.

I liked it more than Red.

Maybe I'm a little too close to be entirely objective on that count, I confess, but I think this one was a little more personal. Red was the sort of character you could project yourself onto. Liv was the sort of character you had to really try to understand.

The story was a rough around the edges, but that's life sometimes, isn't it? Not everything is neat when you want it to be.

If I were waiting for Riley to recover, I might well consider taking the time to transcribe it. But according to the top right corner, it is about 55,000 words, and we don't have that kind of time.

I'm not waiting for Riley to recover again.

Besides, I think a raw novel of that caliber deserves a little more than to be tacked on to the end of a project like this, that already has two authors.

It was fun to work on, though.

I was worried I could never be a writer, because I'm not creative enough. Even talking about myself, my trauma, I didn't feel like it was interesting. Like I was interesting enough to carry it.

But The Creator, for all his faults, taught me one thing.

It's a noble effort to finish other people's stories.

I feel good that I finished this one, even though I didn't start it.

Now it's time to finish something else.

Now, it's time for a decision.

An ending.

That's one of the scariest things about being a writer: choosing the right final note. How do I want this story to end, for instance?

I didn't know.

For a long time I haven't known.

But then I asked it a different way.

When I wrap everything up here, I'm going to get to show the world who I am. I get to reinvent myself.

If I could step out of here as anyone, would I really want it to be as a killer?

Or a hero?

Part 5
Red

An Epilogue

Red Responds: An Interview with Riley Dawson

By Arthur Lewis

The story of The Re-Creator has swept the nation. An obsessed fan of an independent webcomic tried to emulate his favorite villain, kidnapping and torturing three women in the North-Eastern United States. We are lucky enough to have gotten an exclusive interview with the writer of the comic and one confirmed survivor: Riley Elizabeth Dawson.

In my conversation with her she opened up about her traumatic experience, how it ties into her new book, and what the recovery process has been like.

AL: Let me just start on record by saying thank you for your time and willingness to discuss all of this.

RED: Thank you for having me. I've been looking for someone to help me get the word out there.

AL: I think a lot of people have been surprised by your absence in the media. Even with the book coming out last month, there wasn't much of a press tour. You've been a challenging woman to get ahold of.

RED: I was for a little while. I needed some time to myself, to recover, you know? To process everything. To write the book. That helped a lot, just getting the story out there. But once my work was out in the world again, it felt like I could still be doing more to spread the word. I finally feel ready.

AL: Well, as I said, I'm grateful you accepted the invitation. I have a lot of questions for you about the book, and your experience prior to writing it. But I hope you don't mind if I start with a more personal question?

RED: Not at all.

AL: Mrs. Dawson?

Her whole face lights up to be asked about her name. Newspapers have been reporting on 'Riley Langdon' so much that she has become almost a household name at this point. It seems as though I have stumbled across a story in the change that she's more than a little eager to tell.

RED: Yes. Yes! I've gotten married. Just before the release of the book, actually.

AL: Who's the lucky man?

RED: Officer Sam Dawson.

AL: Officer? I feel like there's a story there.

Her smile is so soft and innocent. She looks younger than her thirty years, and hardly seems like the type of woman capable of writing such a lurid comic in the first place.

RED: He's actually the one who found me and brought me in to the hospital, if you can believe it.

AL: Was he really?

RED: He was, he was. He said he was just waiting for me to wake so he could take my statement, but he kept watch over me while I was sleeping. He came to see me after his shifts when I didn't have anyone else by my side. He held my hand while I was trying to remember everything. Eventually, it got to the point I just couldn't imagine being apart from him.

AL: That sounds like something straight out of a great romance.

RED: It does, doesn't it? Though, hopefully not the sort of romance I would write.

AL: Speaking of your writing. Do you mind if we get into it?

RED: Not at all. It's why I'm here.

AL: They say that The Re-Creator was inspired by a webcomic you wrote.

RED: Yes. He was inspired by "The Creator," who I guess you would consider the comic's antagonist. He's the operator of the red room.

AL: What exactly is a red room?

This is a phrase that Mrs. Dawson has used before, and which has come up in several interviews over the course of her career. The publicity of this case has brought attention to the terrible concept, but I'm curious to see how she will describe them given her close, personal connection to the myth.

RED: Well... red rooms don't really exist.

They're just a sort of legend that has been around for ten, maybe fifteen years. They're like chatrooms, but on the deep web. They're very private, very exclusive. And basically, they let you pay to watch a person getting tortured on a sort of livestream. It's all completely anonymous.

The whole thing has been thoroughly debunked, of course. I did a lot of research for my comic that proved that they're not real.

AL: So you didn't experience any of that while you were there?

RED: No, no. I mean... there was... there were bad things that happened. No one wants to hear the gory details of all that, but bad things happened in front of the cameras. I don't doubt that the technology exists to livestream it somewhere. There wasn't enough connection to do it on the deep web, but...

AL: But?

RED: Well, there are some real sickos out there. I think if there's one thing that the Re-Creator has taught us, it's that people are interested in this sort of thing. It scares me some that all the technology basically already exists.

It's not as secure or anonymous as the deep web, obviously, but someone could make a lot of money hosting this sort of thing on the surface web if they had a tech background and a lot of trust for the people in the chat with them.

AL: Let's hope we never see such a thing attempted again. This was bad enough, I'm sure. Can you tell us what it was like, though? Waking up in your own comic?

Mrs. Dawson looks more serious, but resolved to talk about it. She has a quiet strength, even as she contemplates what to say.

RED: It was... I mean, there really are no words for it. I'd seen that room about a hundred times over, from just about every angle while we were working on the comic. But never from the table like that. And it was weird... it was almost like an out-of-body experience. Because Red, the protagonist, had also woken up in such a way during a pivotal moment in the comic. And she was modeled after me, so in a way I'd already seen what I'd look like in that situation, and it was so vivid in my mind that it was still sort of like I was looking down at myself, if that makes sense.

AL: It must have been terrifying.

RED: I have never been so scared in my life. I had no idea what was about to happen to me. How things were going to end.

AL: Did you already know that two other women had been killed?

RED: No. Well, not exactly. I knew one woman had died, a couple states over. I had feared the similarities between how they found her and my comic—which was why I had taken a hiatus.

That hiatus was something I thought about a lot while I was a prisoner. I didn't have any close friends or family. I had a following, but I had basically told them not to expect any word from me. So I knew it would be awhile before anyone thought to look for me. If they ever did. I think that was the scariest part for me, having no one.

AL: And you didn't know about the second victim yet?

RED: Not when I woke up. No.

She looks away so suddenly, and I wonder if I've said something wrong. I fear in the moment that I've triggered a memory too painful for the poor woman. I am about to apologize when she summons the strength required to continue her train of thought.

RED: But I came to know her. He had us at the same time. We were kept gagged, so I didn't get the chance to talk to her. But I felt like we shared something. I felt... very protective of this woman. I felt... responsible for her.

AL: Responsible?

RED: Well, I knew that I was the reason she was suffering. That she was there because of what I wrote.

AL: Can you tell us what happened to her?

RED: That's the hardest part of this whole thing. I don't even know.

AL: Was she still alive when you escaped?

RED: She was. I had knocked him—The Re-Creator—over the head and the first thing I did was go over to her. She was chained down to the floor and I was trying to get her loose, and she was just shaking her head so violently. She kept nodding to the door, and I knew she wanted me to run. But there was a part of me, you know, that just couldn't bear to leave her. It wasn't her fault, what was happening. She didn't deserve to be there.

I remember the last thing I said to her was that I was going to bring back help. That I wasn't going to leave her with him. And even when I was looking back over my shoulder, she was nodding, nodding for me to go.

AL: And that was the last time you ever saw her?

RED: It was the last time I ever saw her.

AL: The newspaper was unclear about what happened after... what happened to them?

RED: Nobody knows. We... no bodies were ever found. The facility was never found.

AL: How is that even possible?

RED: It doesn't seem like it should be, does it? But it was this sort of... I don't want to call it a bunker. But it was underground. The door was small. I was lucky enough to find his truck outside, but I had no idea where I was or what direction to go in. I was hungry and dehydrated, and just so, so scared.

When Officer Dawson—Sam—found me, I had crashed just off to the side of the road. They think I probably passed out behind the wheel.

The police were able to run plates after, which was how they identified The Re-Creator. They found some of Ms. Glasgow's things at his apartment, but that was nearly a two days' drive away from where they'd found me. Even by the time I regained consciousness, I could barely remember how I'd gotten to hospital, let alone any directions I'd taken before the crash.

AL: So they're still looking?

RED: They're still looking. I'm still looking. I promised I wasn't going to leave her there and I won't. I can't. I couldn't live with myself if I weren't doing everything I could do, even if it's not much.

AL: Well, is there anything else you can tell us about her? The second victim?

RED: Red. He called her Red. That was how I knew her.

AL: Do you know how old she might have been?

RED: She had been through hell... and looked a little rough. But I would say younger than me. I wouldn't put her past her mid-twenties.

AL: And what does she look like?

RED: Well, she looked a bit like the character, a bit like me. Actually, after all the reconstructive surgeries I've had, she probably looks more like me than I do these days.

AL: Reconstructive surgeries?

RED: Another reason why I took some time before I accepted any interview requests. When I said I needed to heal, a lot of that was physical. There was emotional stuff too, therapy, support groups, reconnecting with my mother, but yes, there were several surgeries.

Indeed, looking at her, the jagged cuts that we had seen plastered over the internet from her discovery last year seems to have faded into no more than soft, pink lines.

AL: It is remarkable that someone could go through what you've been through and come out the other side changed for the better.

RED: It is for the better, isn't it?

AL: It certainly seems to be. You have a husband, your family, your book.

RED: Yes, yes. My book. *Recreating Red.*

AL: Now, correct me if I'm wrong, but this is the first book you've ever written?

RED: Yes. While I was in recovery, writing it helped me to make sense of everything that had happened. And I wanted to release it, to help me to tell the stories of the other two victims to the extent that I could.

Half of the proceeds are going to the ongoing investigation. 25% is going to Mrs. Glasgow and her family. And 10% is being donated to help the victims of human trafficking.

AL: Well, the book is everywhere right now. It seems as though you're raising good money for all these causes.

RED: I have been truly amazed by the amount of support for this project. Even the artist of the comic offered to do the foreword, and has been great in promoting it.

AL: And do you see much of the artist?

RED: Not so much these days. Maybe, someday. We had talked once about collaborating again, but right now I just feel like I need to be working on my own.

AL: And on that note, I do have just one more question for you.

RED: Of course.

AL: What's next for you? Creatively speaking.

RED: Well... it's a little early to announce this... but I've found a publisher for my first proper novel, Heart-Eater. It's fiction, but I think the world needs that kind of escapism right now.

AL: I think I speak for everyone when I say how inspiring it is to see you thriving. We were all relieved to see your part of the story get a happy ending.

RED: Oh, but my part of the story is just finally beginning.

'Recreating Red' is now available at bookstores and online. It features a foreword by esteemed comic artist and concerned friend, Mila, as well as a touching dedication from Riley herself.

"From one Red to another."

Acknowledgements

I have so many people to thank for the creation of Revenge Arc, starting with the 24hr Novel Challenge on Twitter. I had been wanting to write Riley's story since 2016 and had started and abandoned it countless times over the years, across many formats. When I finally finished a draft of the story it was last year, as part of the challenge. I wrote 50,047 words that weekend and most of them were deleted to bring you this book.

I also have to give tremendous thanks to my good friend, Ghost. She is one of the kindest, most generous people I know generally, but has been a huge supporter of this book in particular. While preparing for the aforementioned challenge I pestered her a lot about whether or not it would be insane to follow this found file idea and she really pushed for it. She was so encouraging after I sent her the first part of the book, and was actually the first one to pitch that it be released with true-to-source formatting (which I did not believed could be done at the time.)

That formatting makes it what it is, and would have been impossible without Archive of the Odd. I was pretty sure I was going to end up having to self-publish this story, and I had no idea how I was going to do any of it on my own. I'm eternally grateful that I didn't have to. The whole team stepped in to bring this thing out of my head and into the world.

Cormack has been so amazing. From our first email where I wrote and asked if it would even be worth pitching something this long, through literally every stage of the creative process. When we turned the manuscript over to be formatted, illustrated and put together I was afraid I'd be totally useless. That's mostly been true, but Cormack introduced me to the team and made me feel included every step of the way.

Elliott has done some master marketing, epic formatting, and contributed to one of the single best work playlists I've ever heard. William has created some of the most stunning, and on-brand movie posters for this project. Bee has worked me through many stages of my impractical costuming whims and helped put together the designs that brought my characters to life. One of those designs was used for gorgeous, full-color comic pages done by Bri who was an absolute pleasure to work with from day one of art commissions.

These are just a handful of examples of the many extra miles the Archive team has put in to make this project a reality. I couldn't begin to count, let alone list, all the extra efforts that have been made for me during production. I don't think a week has passed in the last couple months that I haven't been blown away by the attention to detail that has been afforded to this book.

I'd also like to acknowledge my family, particularly my parents. Thank you for believing in me during the rough years, celebrating with me during the good years, and adopting a new cat every time I leave the state.

I'm also taking this moment to dedicate the book to my 7th grade language arts teacher, Mrs. Skidmore. I had to make up a test during my lunch period one day and she told me that after the trouble she'd had scheduling it, I needed to dedicate my first book to her. I'm pretty sure she was joking, but she also believed that I was going to finish a book someday. She knew I was going to be a writer long before I believed it.

Finally, I just want to thank all the beta readers, ARC readers, and everyone that has already shown support to this project. The response on social media has been so encouraging and I couldn't be more grateful there are readers willing to take a chance on something strange. If you're reading this right now, know that this whole thing was done in part for you.

Sincerely,

Cat

Press Credits

Editorial

CM Baldwin
EV Smith

Copy Editing Team
Julian Stuart

Art

Concept
Bee Olive
Will Taylor

Cover
Grim Poppy
Designs

Illustration
Bri Crozier

Additional Graphics
Cat Voleur, CM Baldwin, EV Smith, Grim Poppy Designs,
Mohamed_hassan (Pixabay), images in public domain

Marketing
Haley Strassburger (@spoonie.reads), CM Baldwin, EV
Smith, Will Taylor

Additional Thank You To...
ARC readers, Tyler Battaglia for assistance with icons,
The Vile Cesspool, Shortwave publishers' chat, and
YOU, the reader!

About the Author

Cat Voleur is a writer of dark fiction with works featured in *Hell Hath Only Fury*, *Livestock*, and *Divergent Terror*. She co-hosts two podcasts; Slasher Radio and This Horror Life. When she is not creating or consuming morbid content, you can most often find her with a small army of rescue felines, pursuing her passion for fictional languages. catvoleur.com

GRIM
POPPY

Cover design services dealing primarily in the
horror genre. Premades, customs, magazine
covers, etc.

Twitter: @grimpoppydesign
Patreon: patreon.com/grimpoppydesign

About the Artist

Bri 'Pi' Crozier is well known for their deep adoration of the macabre. A writer and illustrator with a degree in both, Bri is passionate about the natural cycle of decay and death, finding beauty in how it relates to their experiences as a queer and disabled person. When not writing, painting, or making comics, Bri can be found looking for dead things in Kansas City, where they are pursuing a MFA in creative writing.

Bricrozierart.com
@ear_a_Corn Instagram & Twitter

About the Publisher

Archive of the Odd is a micropress specializing in speculative found fiction, run by Cormack Baldwin. It publishes short fiction in the magazine Archive of the Odd. *Revenge Arc* is its first novella. archiveoftheodd.com

Printed in the USA
CPSIA information can be obtained
at www.ICGtesting.com
JSHW041637050823
46008JS00005B/25

9 798988 482703